PRAIRIE RAIN

PRIMROSE SERIES
BOOK SIX

TANYA RENEE

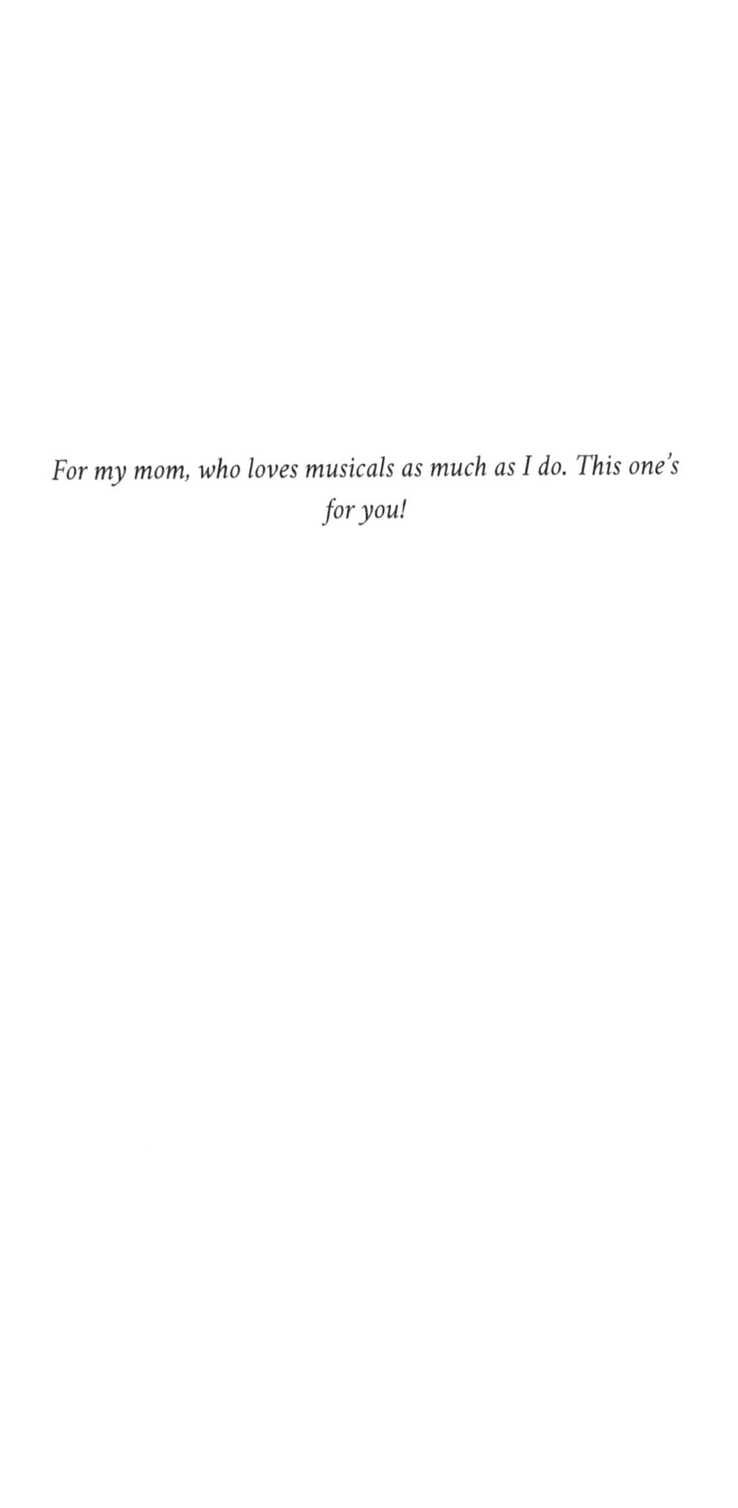

For my mom, who loves musicals as much as I do. This one's for you!

ALSO BY TANYA RENEE

Primrose Series

Prairie Sky

Prairie Nights

Prairie Fire

Prairie Hearts

Prairie Sound

Prairie Rain

Prairie Prestige

With The Band

Finding Direction

Love Notes

PROLOGUE

*D*ee rapped softly on the classroom door as she entered the chemistry lab at Primrose High School. Garrett Smithfield, the resident chemistry teacher, looked up from the test he was grading, and gave her an acknowledging smile as he set his red pen down. "Dee, come on in and grab a seat," he said, gesturing to a student table as he rose and rounded his desk to join her.

Dee took a seat, offering the brother of her best friend, Savanah, a warm, kind smile. Having grown up an only child, Garrett had become like a brother to her over the years, and she appreciated their close relationship.

Dee glanced around the classroom, taking in the beakers, flasks, and test tubes set up along the far wall and catching on a big poster near the front that said "Chemistry. It's like magic but real". Dee laughed, loving his weird science guy sense of humor. Her gaze returned to Garrett as she commented with a cheeky smirk, "Nice digs, nerd."

"My home away from home," he replied with a grin,

holding his arms out proudly as he turned the conversation back to her. "Now tell me, how was the interview with Doris?"

Dee let her eyes fall downcast, running her hands over her pencil skirt to smooth it out, taking a moment to pick some lint clinging to the fabric, her face serious and stoic. Garrett's mouth turned into a frown, a look of disappointment in his eyes as he waited in anticipation for her response. She slowly lifted her head and met his uncertain gaze, a twinkle flashing in their midnight depths and a smile curving her lips up into a smile.

Garrett hesitantly returned her smile, as the realization that she, in true Dee fashion, was stalling for dramatic effect. "You got the job, didn't you?" he asked.

"Of course I did!" she exclaimed, jumping up from the chair with excitement. He rose with her, putting out his arms for a hug. She slipped her arms around him giving him an affectionate squeeze. "Thank you so much for the referral, Garrett! Becoming the drama teacher here at Primrose High is a dream come true."

"Anything for my sis from another miss," he said with a laugh as he held her out at arm's length. "When do you start?"

"I start in January, right after Christmas break, and the best part is I get to decide on the Spring musical." She replied, the joy and excitement bursting with her words.

"Excellent! Seriously, Dee you're going to love working here."

CHAPTER 1

Devine Jones loved the stage. Everything about it filled her with joy and happiness. The costumes, the lights, the audience, the applause. Every little detail that goes into a successful production, simply thrilling. There was nothing more satisfying than pouring your heart and soul into a role, taking a bow, and getting a standing ovation. She had always been drawn to the stage, acting in her blood. With her mother a stage actress until she had Dee and her father an accomplished actor as well, quite simply, it was part of her DNA.

Having never known her father, she grew up an only child to a single mother. During her childhood, finances were always tight, and they never had the money to put her in acting camps or drama classes. That didn't stop her, though. Having known from a very early age that she wanted to be in the spotlight, her mother brought her to auditions and by the time she was five years old, she had been cast in a national commercial. From there, her passion for acting and the stage became clear to her mother, so she encouraged her to take part in every opportunity she could to get up in front of people, whether it be in the community or school theatre. Dee had dozens of productions under her belt, so when she received a university scholarship, she decided on a major in education and a minor in theatre, with the dream of one day combining both into her dream job. Now here she was, the drama teacher, creative director extraordinaire of Primrose High School, and she couldn't be happier. Three months into her position at Primrose High and it still felt like a dream to her. As a high school with a long legacy of exceptional dramas and musicals coming from their small-town stage, Mrs. Doris Newman spent over 30 years bringing out the talent of the best and the brightest of Primrose, and now Dee had the honor of filling her illustrious shoes.

Dee glanced in her full-length mirror, straightening out her bright yellow blouse and black wide leg trousers, feeling every bit the cool young and sophisticated drama teacher. Tying her crochet braids off her face in a simple knot, she surveyed herself in the mirror as she slipped on a pair of gold hoop earrings. Taking one last look at her outfit, accessories and make-up, she smiled. *You got this, girl*; she reminded herself and confidently walked out of her bedroom, ready to tackle the day ahead.

Today was the first day back after spring break and she was eager to get to the school to get ready for auditions later that morning. The spring musical season was upon them, and she was beyond excited to bring the Gene Kelly classic, *Singin' in the Rain* to the Primrose stage in only two short months. She had her work cut out for her, but as ever, Dee was up for the challenge.

Entering the main living area of her new condo, she looked around at the high-end finishes of her open concept kitchen, and around the spacious living room and dining area. She loved this corner condo, and from the first visit to the show unit last summer till this past week when she was able to move in, she couldn't believe she finally had a space she could truly call her own. Plus, the location couldn't be more perfect. On the west side of Primrose she was just down the street from her best friend Savanah and within walking distance from the school.

Glancing out the floor to ceiling patio doors of her condo, the skies were clear, the grey rain clouds from the day before having dissipated, leaving room for only bright blue and wispy white clouds. It appeared to be a gorgeous, cool and crisp spring morning. *A perfect day to walk to work.* Making her way to the front entrance, she slipped on her good walking shoes and her favorite cropped leather jacket as she reached for her large boho bag and slipped it over her body. An umbrella hung on a hook in her closet, and she glanced at it debating if she should grab it. The debate was a short one, as the weather this time of year was unpredictable. Sliding it into her bag, she took one last look at herself in the front entrance mirror, appraised herself one last time and unlatched her door.

Although it was the beginning of April, it was unseasonably warm for this time of year, making it as good a day as any to start her new walking routine. April in Manitoba tended to be wet and rainy and quite often there was still snow either on the ground or in the fore-cast. Although it had rained on and off over the weekend, she was confident her walk to the school would be a pleasant one.

Locking her condo door, she strode towards the eleva-tor, straightening her large boho bag across her body into a comfortable position. The elevator of the six-floor condo building came quickly, and she got on as she pulled out her ear buds and slipped them into her ears. The soundtrack of *Singin' in the Rain* came through, making her smile, the plan for today filling her chest with warmth and anticipation. She loved this musical and couldn't wait to bring it to life.

Exiting the elevator, she passed the workout room, glancing in and thinking she needed to check it out soon as strode past the building office and mailbox wall. Exiting the building into the brisk spring morning, she stopped, breathing in deeply the smell of fresh dirt and rain. Humming to the soundtrack as she walked down the sidewalk, the sun was shining, the birds were chirping cheerfully as Gene Kelly, Debbie Reynolds and Donald O'Conner sang out "Good Morning" and she couldn't help but think, *what a good morning indeed.*

Reaching the juncture of her street and Main Street, she waited patiently at the corner to cross as a few vehi-cles passed and, seeing it was clear, she happily strode to the other side of the street. Large puddles lined the street, some large enough to overflow the curb but not reach the sidewalk. She lifted her trousers so she could skip over a puddle and make her way to the sidewalk on the other side. Just as she cleared the puddle, a large pickup truck turned from Main Street, splashing up the rainwater drenching her with the spray. She stood there on the edge of the road, hands up, a look of disbelief on her face as she took in her ruined pants and blouse soaked with cold, muddy water. The truck braked with a loud squeal on the other side of the intersection and the driver's side door flew open.

"Are you okay?" a rich deep voice called out as she stood there in shock at what had just happened.

"No!" she snapped, her once cheerful mood suddenly teeming with frustration as she took in the disaster that was her outfit and pulled out her ear buds, angrily stuffing them into the pocket of her jacket.

"Ma'am, I'm so sorry. I didn't see you there and…" the voice was now closer to her.

"You were going too fast!" she exclaimed with a huff as she glanced up into the face of the man attempting to apologize. Her glare was met with the most gorgeous ocean blue eyes and, much to her own internal protest, her frustration and anger softened towards the handsome man standing before her.

"I was probably going too fast," he replied, raising his hands, his brows furrowed as he took in her dirty wet clothes.

"Probably?" she asked, a soft indignation in her tone as she took him in. The man in front of her was the epitome of tall, dark, rugged, and handsome. His hair was sexily messy and curled out at the ends haphazardly. He had a dark 5 o'clock shadow that covered his strong jawline and bewitching blue eyes. He wore a plaid work jacket, a Henley shirt that stretched over his long lean torso and faded boot cut jeans with steel toe boots. He looked like he was either a farmer or off to work hard labor on a job site.

"You're right, I was going too fast. Again, I'm so very sorry," he said now at her side, meeting her gaze, a sincere look of apology on his impossibly handsome face. "Wait here, I probably have a towel in the back of the truck," he said, turning from her and rushing over to his truck, opening a storage box in the bed. Pulling out a beach towel, he rushed back over and handed it to her.

She accepted it graciously and tried to wipe down her soaked pants, groaning at the mud on her beautiful yellow blouse. "I need to go home and change." She said, shaking her head in defeat and handing him back the soiled towel.

"Are you close? I can give you a lift," he offered, sincerity in his tone as his eyes locked on hers. "Honestly, that's the least I can do after I completely ruined your clothes."

Dee prided herself on being street smart and taking rides from random strangers was not something she was in the habit of doing. However, seeing the kindness in the eyes of this handsome stranger, her intuition told her he was harmless. Besides, she had taken self-defense classes and knew at least 15 ways to maim or disable him if she needed to.

She squinted, giving him one more scrutinizing look before she answered. "I'd appreciate that. I just live in the new condo complex at the end of the street."

"I live there too. I'm Jaxon Isley." he said, putting out his hand to her in greeting.

Dee slowly accepted his hand and met his gaze, his

breathtaking blue eyes catching the morning light and making them twinkle as a sweet smile tugged at his lips. *Dear Lord, those are some sexy lips.* His smile deepened, causing his eyes to crease endearingly at the corners as he held onto her hand a beat longer than was necessary. A surge of warmth ran through her body at the feel of her hand in his and she had to remind herself that she was really upset by this situation she found herself in. Dee met his smiling eyes, and that was it. Any anger or frustration seemed to melt away by the warmth that radiated from his gaze. Dee shook her head, trying to get her bearings as she replied. "I'm Devine Jones."

"Well, Ms. Jones, shall we go?" he asked, gesturing over to his truck. She nodded, and he watched as she jumped over the puddle again and walked over to the passenger side. On the truck door, she noticed the Isley Construction decal, which was the company that she dealt with when she purchased her condo. Opening the door, she climbed in as he got into the cab next to her.

"Isley Construction. Is that your company?" she asked, slipping on her seat belt, and giving him a surveying side eye as he did a U-turn and turned down her street, heading towards the condominiums.

"Yes." he replied, glancing over at her. "And where were you headed this morning?"

"The high school. I'm the new drama teacher at Primrose High." she replied, chin high and proud.

"Ah! I heard Mrs. Newman retired." he said with a look of nostalgia on his face. "I always enjoyed being part of her productions when I was in high school. You're looking at none other than Curly in the 2009

Primrose production of "Oklahoma"." he shared with a cheesy grin.

Dee instantly liked his smile. Bright white, with one tooth off to the left that was a little crooked and made him look kind of boyish, even though she was sure he was well into his 30s. It was an endearing imperfection. She grinned back, feeling surprisingly relaxed around this man she just met. "Handsome young cowboy, I can see it," she commented with a hint of flirtation in her voice.

Noticing, his lips tugged up in a sweet smile as he turned into the parking lot and pulled up to the front door of the condo. Putting the vehicle into park, he turned to her. "I'll wait here for you and make sure to get you to work. Take as much time as you need. I'm not in a rush to get anywhere."

"Because you're the boss?" Dee asked cheekily. Jaxon smirked, and he nodded as she got out of the truck. Glancing over her shoulder, she flashed the handsome country boy a smile and slipped through the front door of the building, feeling his eyes on her as she went.

Jaxon sat there, watching the beautiful Ms. Jones disappear into the building. Letting out a low whistle, he ran a hand over his scruffy chin. *She is gorgeous.* Her midnight-colored eyes, like nothing he had ever seen before. Those high enviable cheekbones, full plump lips and a smile that made her cheeks indent into the sexiest dimples. *Damn.* It had been a long time since he met a woman that intrigued him, and the ebony beauty that was just in his truck was beyond intriguing.

At 37, Jaxon would describe his past love life as a story line out of a soap opera. As a high school baseball star, president of the student council his senior year, and declared the most popular guy at Primrose High in the yearbook, he was never lacking for dates and girls on his arm. Then, being drafted right out of high school to a Major League farm team, he found himself playing Minor League baseball in Buffalo, New York, where he met his now ex-wife, Leah. Leah was a blonde, blue-eyed beauty from New York City, whom he met at a nightclub on a night out with some teammates. Tall and svelte, Leah had a model's body and was very glamorous. Nothing like the small-town girls he was used to. She immediately had her sights on Jaxon, and he was the envy of all his friends and teammates. Two years into their relationship, he proposed, and they married in a large, lavish wedding, with him vowing to give her everything her heart desired and more. Only a year into their marriage, things started to get rocky. Leah's demands of him had become overwhelming as she spent money like he was in the big league, trying to maintain a lifestyle far beyond their means and racking up debt they couldn't afford. After 4 years of marriage when he was yet again passed up by the Major Leagues, she told him she wanted a divorce as she was in love with one of his teammates who had been brought up the year prior to the majors and whom he later found out had been sleeping with his wife behind his back. Being thrown into a messy divorce, he emerged not only financially ruined but left with a battered and bruised ego and heart. He tried to move on after his divorce, but the game became a reminder of his shambled life, so he walked away from his baseball dreams, returned to Canada to be closer to family, and tried to pick up the shattered pieces of his life.

After a few months of wallowing, Jaxon's parents encouraged him to go back to school. He attended business school, successfully helped a friend flip houses, and started doing odd renovation jobs on the side. With his degree in hand and extensive experience under his belt, he decided to open his own construction company, opening an office in his hometown of Primrose. Building his clientele and taking all the profits he had saved up from his many projects as well as contributions from investors, he purchased land on the west side of town, to build the first condo building in Primrose. Proud of how he turned his financial situation around, he was now able to provide for himself and his employees. Jaxon had a good life and everything he could need or want. At least almost everything. Eight years after his divorce, his love life was in dire need of resuscitation. He hadn't so much as dated since his divorce, and at this point, had concluded that he likely never would.

Now, here he was, on his way to the office, when a chance encounter with a stunningly beautiful woman made him consider the possibilities. Jaxon never considered himself to have a type. However, it wasn't lost on him just now that the lovely Ms. Jones wasn't like any other woman that had piqued his interest. Strikingly beautiful, with flawless brunet skin, and a smile that could stop a man in his tracks, Jaxon found himself feeling just a little awestruck by her.

The doors to the condo building opened, breaking him from his thoughts and Devine emerged, making his jaw slack at the sight of her. She had changed into a red pencil skirt that hugged her generous curves and a white blouse that crisscrossed modestly over her upper body to accentuate her narrow waist and abundant chest. Her same rocker style black leather jacket she had on before finished off her new outfit and she had added a bright red lipstick to her already beautiful face, making her full lips look luscious and kissable. She got into the cab, sliding in carefully, and offering him a devious smile. Realizing he was staring; Jaxon blinked and reciprocated her grin as he stuttered on his words. "You…ah… you clean up nice, Ms. Jones."

"Please call me Dee and thank you. I kind of liked what I was wearing, but some cowboy in his big old truck had other ideas." She teased, playfully cocking her eyebrow at him.

Jaxon ran his hand over the scruff on his chin, shook his head, then turned to face her and held up his hand. "I, Jaxon Isley, vow from this day forward to always look out for beautiful women crossing the street."

"Beautiful? Are you trying to charm me into forgiving you, Mr. Isley?" she asked, her midnight eyes twinkling with her question.

A slow smile curled his lips at her inquisition, loving how she so confidently and flirtatiously bantered with him. "Yes, you heard me correctly. You are beautiful and yes, I was hoping for some absolution for my crime. Call me J. That's what my friends call me."

Dee stared at him for a moment, her eyes fixed with his and ensnaring him with their hold. Then she graced him with that show stopping smile and let out a little raspy laugh. The throating sound running through his body like an electrical charge through a tuning fork, jolting him with awareness. *I need to hear so much more of that sexy little laugh.*

"You and I are friends now?" she asked, pointing between them.

"Sure." he answered, very much enjoying the easy back and forth between them.

Dee tapped her index finger on her chin, narrowing her eyes as she considered giving a friendship with him some thought, before she turned to face him, offering Jaxon a devilish grin and answered, "Okay, then J, aka Cowboy, we can be friends and I'll forgive you on one condition." She proposed, holding one finger up to him with a conspiring smile on her gorgeous face.

"What's that?" he asked, his eyes meeting hers with amused curiosity.

Her eyes flashed at him playfully as her grin widened. "You'll volunteer to build the sets for the Spring Musical Production at the high school."

Well played. Jaxon grinned, wanting so much more time with this intriguing woman as he replied, "Consider it done."

CHAPTER 2

The excitement in the drama room was palpable. The anxious eyes of all the students were on her, making Dee's heart race with the mounting excitement as she held up the coveted cast list.

"Now, before I post this on the bulletin board, I want to say I'm overwhelmed by the talent in this room." She beamed, holding her hand to her heart. "Your auditions were all fantastic and you should be very proud of how you all got out of your comfort zones to not only sing but dance for your auditions." The students all glanced around at each other, offering smiles, a collective murmur sounding in the large open classroom before she continued. "Now, if you didn't get a main role, don't be disheartened. We need background actors and students in the chorus to make these productions incredible. Every part, big or small, is important." With that, Dee strode over to the bulletin board, pinned the cast list to it, turned and nodded to her students, ducking out of the way with a laugh as they stampeded towards the list. The sound of cheers and jeers echoed in the large room, most faces happy, some slightly disappointed, but all in all, a positive response to her casting. Giving them a few minutes to chatter amongst themselves, she took in the hum of excitement in the room and smiled at her students. Putting her hand up to quiet them down, she took control of the room. "Okay everyone, take a seat." Picking up the stack of scripts, she spent hours photocopying. She smiled as she passed them out to her eager students. "Here is the script. Know your part and work on memorizing as much as you can. *Singin' in the Rain* is an iconic musical and I think with the talent in this room, we're going to wow Primrose this season." she added. "I'll be bringing in a few friends from my stage days to help with your vocals and choreography and I'll be your acting coach and director."

"Ms. Jones?" asked a pretty blonde girl Dee recognized from the Senior class who she cast as the lead Kathy Selden. "Is there anything else other than memorizing our lines that we can do to prepare?"

"Great question." She replied with an approving smile. "This Friday we'll all gather in this room to watch the 1952 screen adaptation of Singin in the Rain, starring legends Gene Kelly and Debbie Reynolds. I want you to take in the beauty of 1940s Hollywood and take a partic-ular interest in the actors that are playing your part. I want you to get those iconic songs stuck in your head because you'll be hearing a lot of them over the next two months. Truly, I think you will fall in love with this musical as much as I have."

Her students' smiles were wide, and excited chatter rose echoing off the walls, that once the retractable wall was removed, served as the stage for the production. Dee glanced at the clock on the wall and, seeing it was almost the end of the day, turned her attention back to her students and declared, "You are all dismissed and enjoy reading those scripts! If you have any questions, you know where to find me." She said with a wink. "Rehearsals officially start on Monday."

All the students excitedly filed out of the classroom as the Gym Teacher, Anders Barick, slipped into the room between the students. Anders was Dee's age, stood about five foot ten, had a bulky muscular build and looked more like a wrestler than a high school gym teacher. He had floppy blonde hair and hazel eyes and was undeniably good-looking. The problem, however, was that he knew it. Ego and arrogance oozing off him, there was absolutely nothing humble about Anders. It had been obvious since day one that he was used to getting what he wanted and since she started at the school in January; he had his sights zoned in on Dee.

"Hey there, Dee Dee!" he said smarmily, his voice dripping with flirtation as his eyes drifted down to her ample chest. Dee internally rolled her eyes and feigned him a smile. He strode over to her casually, his t-shirt looking far too small as it stretched over his bulging muscular chest, and his athletic shorts clinging for dear life to narrow hips and impressive tree trunk legs. Taking a seat in her desk chair, he blatantly looked her up and down with approval, settling his gaze on her ass. "You look nice," he said, enunciating the word "nice" in a tone he probably thought was sexy, but for Dee was missing the mark. "Got that whole hot teacher vibe going."

As annoying as Anders was, Dee could handle a guy like him. In fact, she had dealt with a lot worse. Even though she had zero interest in him, she had to give him props for his confidence and persistence. He had asked her out every week, since she had started at Primrose High and she was pretty sure that was why he was here now, taking up her space and annoying her.

"I understand you need to use my gym for musical practice." He informed, his voice drawl and cocky. "I guess I could allow you to use my space on one condition."

Here it comes. Dee turned to face him, folding her arms over her chest and narrowing her eyes conspiratorially, as she replied, "What condition?"

"You go out with me Saturday night," he replied, flashing her a sly smile.

"Did you proposition Mrs. Newman like that?" she asked, volleying back pointedly.

Anders let out a huge guffaw as he replied, "That old bird she wishes."

Dee rolled her eyes in exasperation. *What a jerk.* "I'm pretty sure my use of the gym is unconditional, and the principal would agree. Besides, I already have a date on Saturday night so..." *A little white lie couldn't hurt, right?*

Anders straightened up in her chair and squinted his eyes at her as he asked, "Who are you going out with?"

"My love life isn't any of your business, Anders." she replied, flashing him a feigned a smile as she grabbed her remaining scripts and slid them into her bag. He rose from her chair, and she was met with an agitated glare, just as the end of day bell rang, breaking the mounting tension that was building in the room. "Well, another day is done." Dee chimed, pulling her jacket from the back of her chair and slipping it on. "Have a nice night, Anders!" she exclaimed, turning her back and giving him a two-finger wave as she exited her classroom.

A satisfied smile on her face, justifiably proud of how she handled the latest encounter with the egotistical gym teacher, Dee got to the outside doors of the school and groaned as she looked outside at what had turned into a cold, windy and wet afternoon. *Damn you, Manitoba, with all this spring rain.* As Dee zipped up her jacket and she berated herself for her lack of foresight as to today's forecast. She reached into her large bag, pulled out the compact umbrella she stuffed in there the other day, and walked through the door, lingering by the overhang to open it. Most of the buses had already gone and only about a half dozen students lingered under the overhang, waiting for their rides.

"Good night, Ms. Jones." a 10th grade boy from her morning class called out as she stepped out onto the wet pavement.

"Good night, Sam," she called back with a smile.

She really liked her students at Primrose High. So far, they were great kids and all were super enthusiastic about the arts. Having taken term positions and substituting for years since getting her education degree, she felt like she had seen it all. Students of every background and situation. Some schools were diverse, and in some schools, she was the only person of color to walk through the doors. Some schools had poor leadership, the kids running the school more than the administration and teachers, and some schools were run like a tight ship. Primrose High

School, although small, had excellent leadership, high academics, winning sports teams and was known for having an outstanding arts program. Dee couldn't have hoped for a better place to teach.

Crossing the street, Dee walked past the fire station and onto the residential part of Main Street, the rain coming down steadily in big cold droplets. Suddenly the wind picked up, bringing a chill that promised that the rain could turn to sleet or snow, and Dee picked up her pace, trying to use her umbrella to shield her, failing miserably. She groaned as the rain hit her face and she felt the cold climb up her spine, settling in as a bitter chill. She was almost at the corner when she glanced at the street, just as a familiar truck pulled over to the curb and the window rolled down.

Jaxon Isley's handsome face greeted her like a knight in shining armor as he ordered, "Get in the truck, Dee."

Dee hesitated a beat as she wasn't one to take an order from anyone, let alone a man, but since this weather was insane, and she was seriously scolding herself for not checking the forecast that morning she wasn't going to turn him down. Hopping over a puddle, she opened the passenger side door as she closed her umbrella, shook it out, and got inside. The cab was blowing hot air, the contrast from the cold outside making goosebumps rise on her skin and her teeth start to chatter.

Jaxon took her in a moment, his eyes locked on her face and brows drawn together in concern, as he asked, "Cold?"

"Yeah." she said as shivers racked her body and she tucked her wet braids behind her ears, pulling up the collar of her leather jacket to try to grasp any semblance of warmth.

"Hold on," he said, unbuckling her seatbelt, turning, and reaching behind the seat. As he reached, his Henley shirt rose past the waist of his jeans, showing the v-cut at his hip, and Dee swallowed as her eyes traced the happy trail, disappearing into his jeans. The heat of him in her personal space made her pulse quicken instantly, and she had to suck in a breath, letting it slowly out to try to tamper down her attraction to him. Producing a plaid jacket that matched the one he had on, he returned to his seat and handed it to her. "Here, this will be a lot warmer than your jacket," he said.

Dee took the offered jacket and gave him a grateful smile as she slipped out of her cold wet leather jacket and slipped on the thick insulated plaid one. Instant warmth spread through her body, making her feel like she was being wrapped in a hug. Tucking her nose into the collar, she inhaled deeply, the woodsy manly smell enveloping her senses and awakening her libido. *They need to bottle this scent.* Settling into the warm and cozy feel of the soft flannel material and quilted interior, she glanced down to see the Isley Construction logo and looked up, meeting Jaxon's twinkling blue eyes. That endearing smile curved on his lips as he commented, "Looks good on you."

"Feels good on me," she volleyed as she cocked an eyebrow at him and grinned. "You realize you're never getting it back now, right?"

His eyes flashed and his smile deepened with mischief and mirth as he replied, "I would never dream of asking for it back."

"Good." she said, reaching for her seatbelt and bringing it over her body to fasten it. Curling her fingers around the label of the jacket, she wrapped it snuggly around her and smiled contentedly. "Now take me home, Cowboy."

* * *

PULLING into the condo parking lot, Jaxon parked in his assigned spot and looked out the windshield as the rain came down hard, going sideways with the wind.

"I think you saved me, in the nick of time." Dee commented with a laugh. "Damn, it turned quickly."

"Spring can be unpredictable. I'm just glad I was driving by," he replied with a sweet smile. "I sent the construction crew home early because of the turning weather and was just heading home from the office."

"Lucky me." Dee rasped sexily, gracing him with a wink.

Jaxon liked the way she replied to him with a hint of sass and flirtation in her tone. *That was flirtation, right?* Jaxon internally questioned, realizing how long it had been since he was on the receiving end of such coquettish responses.

"Do you make it a habit of rescuing damsels in distress or is it just me?" she continued with a teasing smile curving her lips.

"Just you," he responded without hesitation, feeling emboldened by their flirty banter.

Dee's eyes flashed with something he hadn't seen in a long time. *Is she interested in me?* He was certainly interested in her. The realization of that made him pause as he met her gorgeous gaze and a surge of electric attraction passed between them. Dee broke their eye contact, an obvious deflection as she leaned forward towards the truck radio and glanced back at him. "Do you mind?"

He gestured for her to go ahead, and she pressed the button turning on the radio. A country tune blasted through the speakers as they both leaned back, listening for a moment, the song talking about a guy in love with his tractor. They glanced at each other, and both burst into laughter at the absurdity of the song as she asked playfully, "Do you own a tractor, Cowboy?"

"No, but I'm sure if I did, I would sing about it." he deadpanned.

Dee laughed, that raspy lilt which he found unbelievably sexy causing his pulse to quicken and jeans to tighten painfully. "You wouldn't sing about a girl? Perhaps a girlfriend or...wife? she asked curiously, her bold question obviously strategic in nature.

She is interested, and she wants to know if I am otherwise attached. "No girlfriend or wife. No special woman in my life," he answered, pausing to see her reaction.

A grin slowly curled her lips up, her sexy dimples indenting her cheeks as her midnight eyes danced with approval.

Jaxon mirrored her grin, his thoughts drifting to how much he wanted to reach out and run his hand down the side of her face. Trace his fingertips down those beautiful cheekbones and into those devilish dimples. Instead, he cleared his throat, trying to dismiss his thoughts as he asked, "What kind of music do you like?"

"My tastes are pretty diverse," she replied. "I like pop, rock, R & B, at least that's mostly what I listen to. I grew up listening to a lot of Motown and I love soundtracks from musicals."

"What's your favorite musical soundtrack?" he asked with genuine interest.

"Hands down, *Dream Girls*." she replied brightly. "I'm named after Loretta Devine, an actress from the original 1980s Broadway cast."

"Your parents were Broadway fans?" he asked curiously.

"Both were actors." She answered. "My mom quit acting when she had me and my dad, honestly, I have no idea. He could still be acting for all I know. He's never been a part of my life. My mom raised me on her own."

Jaxon took in her answer, thinking he admired the way she shared so matter of fact, no sadness in her voice over not having a present father and being raised by a single mother. Such a contrast from the way he grew up with a bustling household of five boys and parents that had been married for 50 years. *I want to know more.* Jaxon felt like a sponge taking in all this information about Dee and cataloguing in his head what he already knew about her. She really was intriguing and not like any other woman he had ever met before.

"You are really interesting, Dee." he commented with sincerity. "I like talking with you."

Dee smiled and leaned back in her seat, taking in his comment as her eyes drifted back to the world outside again, the rain slowly turning to sleet and coming down in thick flakes making the outside look more like a winter wonderland than a spring day. Both sat there for a few minutes, in quiet contemplation, watching the mini spring snowstorm swirl around them.

Dee turned to face him fully, breaking their reverie, a look of slight apprehension in her eyes as a question tumbled out in a flurry. "Do you want to come over for dinner tonight? I was going to cook pasta."

Jaxon sat up straighter, surprised by the invitation, his heart thrumming as he took in the beautiful woman in front of him. He wanted to know so much more about her and didn't want their conversation right now to end, so he replied, "Yeah, that would be nice. Can I bring anything?"

"Just your appetite. I always cook far too much food." She replied with a laugh before she met his gaze, her smile bright. "And I enjoy talking with you, too."

Warmth filling his chest, Jaxon glanced out the windshield at the storm outside before he turned back to her. "Shall we chance it?"

"We shall." She replied, grabbing her bag and slipping it over her body as she reached for the door handle. "Are you ready?"

Jaxon nodded, and they both opened their doors, hopped out of the truck into the wind and freezing rain. They both ran towards the front entrance of the building, their laughter trailing after them as they slid inside quickly. Still laughing they both shook off the wet snow and shared a smile.

"6 p.m.?" she asked.

"Sounds good," he replied, walking with her towards the elevator. They both got in and Dee reached out to press the 6th floor. A grin tugged at his lips as leaned against the wall, making no move towards the elevator buttons. Dee glanced up at him, her eyebrow raised in question as he answered, "Looks like we both live on the top floor."

She let out a little ironic laugh. "I'm #64. And you?"

"#62" he replied with smiling eyes. "Same side, opposite corners. I guess we're neighbors."

"I guess we are." She replied, mirthful at this twist of fate, as the elevator opened, and they stepped out onto their floor, her turning to the left as he turning to the right, both stopping at their respective doors glancing each other's way. With one last flash of that gorgeous, dimpled smile, she melodically drawled. "See you at 6 p.m. Cowboy."

CHAPTER 3

*D*ee slipped into her condo and took a deep breath, letting it out slowly as wrapped her arms around herself, savoring the warmth of Jaxon's flannel jacket. Inhaling deeply, she let the woodsy scent lingering on the material swirl around her senses and she sighed. It had been a hot minute since she met someone that interested her as much as the ruggedly handsome Jaxon Isley. Yet with just two brief encounters, she found herself fantasizing about biting Jaxon's bottom lip and running her fingers through his mess of sexily disheveled dark hair. Then there was his body. A warm flush ran through her at the thought. He was so lean and tall, an athlete's body, and she found herself wanting to slide her hand under his Henley to feel his taut stomach and to trace that delicious V with her fingertips. *Sexy is not an adequate description for him. Yummy or perhaps scrumptious?* She shook her head and let out a raspy laugh. *I better stop.*

Dee slipped out of the magical jacket, took one last self-indulgent inhale, sighed and hung it in her front entrance closet. She tucked away her purse and shoes before entering the main space of her condo. Hands on her hips, she gave the space a quick survey. Pretty much everything had been put away from her move, with only her bookshelf standing empty and a few more boxes in the corner left for her to unpack containing some of her most prized possessions, her favorite books and scripts from past productions.

She turned, walked down the hallway to her bedroom and pulled out her favorite pair of comfortable boyfriend jeans, a bright blue fitted V-neck t-shirt, and a long oversized colorful striped cardigan, changing into them quickly. Entering her ensuite, she pulled her braids back, gathering them on top of her head, fashioning them into a messy bun before she touched up her makeup and made her way to the kitchen to start dinner. Pulling out a package of chicken thighs from the fridge, and a cutting board from the cupboard, she set to work dicing the chicken into bite-size pieces and was just washing her hands when a knock sounded at the door. Glancing at the clock, which read 5:45 p.m., and she smiled knowingly. Someone was eager and the thought of that made her self-admittedly a little bemused. Striding to the door, she opened it to find Jaxon looking effortlessly handsome, dressed in low slung faded jeans, an evergreen V-neck sweater and just in his sock feet. His lack of shoes made her smile as who needs shoes when you literally live a breath away? Looking like he had just showered, his hair slightly damp and, as expected, sexily mussed up, he held out a bottle of white wine to her. Taking it from him, her fingers touched his and that palpable surge of electricity once again made its appearance known. She glanced up at him through her long lashes, his woodsy cologne swirling around her making her feel lightheaded and woozy. *Has a man ever made you feel this intoxicated?*

"Thank you." She rasped on a breath. "C'mon in. You're early. I was just about to start cooking."

Jaxon stepped inside and followed her into the kitchen as he replied, "I figured I could help you."

"You cook?" she asked, glancing at him over her shoulder as she went around the island towards the stove.

"I'm going to be 38 in May, and I've lived on my own for a long time, so I better know how to cook," he replied with a laugh. "My mom made sure all of us boys could survive without her home cooking. We're all very self-sufficient."

I like that. Dee nodded her head with approval as she replied. "Impressive. And now I know more about you. You're 10 years older than me; you have brothers, and you're a proud mama's boy."

"Check, check and check," he replied, making check marks in the air, then leaning against the island with his hands behind him resting on his palms. "10 years younger, eh?"

"I just turned 28 a few weeks ago." She said, meeting his mesmerizing blue gaze, trying to read if their age difference bothered him. Dee had always had a thing for men older than her and if someone looked at her dating history, it was common for her to date men 10-15 years her senior. She grinned and, not seeing even a sign of a flinch at this information, turned to pull out a skillet and pot from the cupboard. "If you insist on helping, perhaps I can get you to start the pasta and I'll make the sauce."

"Can do," he replied, taking the pot from her and bringing it to the sink to fill it with water.

They worked together side by side, stealing glances and coy smiles as they cooked, dangling the thrill of mutual attraction between them. An invisible pull kept drawing Dee closer as she found herself brushing against him at every turn. Jaxon mirrored her, with a hand on her shoulder, a brush of her hip, seemingly small innocent touches, making her sizzle from the all-consuming manly heat of him in her personal space. Everything about this gorgeous man making her thoughts cloud over with lust. Reaching for the Cajun spice, she glanced up at him coquettishly, questioning and innuendo dripping from her tone as she asked, "Do you like spice?"

"I can handle a lot of spice," he replied, his voice taking on a husky edge, a sexy smile tugging at his lips.

Correct answer. Have I got spice for you Cowboy!

"Good, because I am. I mean, this dish is very spicy," she replied, internally groaning at her blatant flirtation but choosing at that moment to jump in feet first.

Jaxon's smile deepened, and his eyes crinkled with mirth and appreciation. *He understood exactly what you said, and he liked it. He liked it a lot.*

* * *

WHAT ON EARTH is this woman doing to me? Jaxon took in her comment, his body awakening from far too long a slumber. Just being around Dee in her space was testing his resolve at a rapid pace. All he wanted was to lift her onto the counter, settle himself between her luscious thighs, then kiss those full gorgeous lips senselessly. He had never experienced such a quick and discernable attraction to a woman before. Even with his ex, he was undoubtedly attracted to her, but it wasn't an insatiable need to kiss and touch her. Slow burn was his usual modus operandi, so this powerful pull to the delectable Ms. Jones was hot-wiring his brain and confusing his heart.

He cleared his throat and asked huskily, "Do you have a strainer? The pasta is done."

Dee fished out a strainer from a corner cabinet and turned to hand it to him. She looked up to meet his gaze, her stunning eyes betraying her desire as his hand brushed her. The spread of warmth and fiery attraction surged through him, crackling and sizzling. Shaking his head to clear the lust filled thoughts populating in his head, he pulled himself away as he took the pot of pasta to the sink to drain it and put the pasta back in the pot, returning it to the stove where Dee was stirring the now finished sauce. She lifted the skillet and poured the creamy sauce over the pasta; the heat washing over both of their faces, creating a thin sheen of sweat on their skin. His eyes caught on her, and she glanced up at him, both of their breaths coming out quicker in the cloud of steam around them. Her eyes never leaving his, she set down the skillet with an awkward clatter. Like a magnet, they drew together, bridging any distance between their bodies and he reached for her face, cupping her cheek, his palm caressing the soft skin and fingertips tracing her cheekbone, dipping into her sexy dimple. Body pressed close to his, she raised her chin to him, her eyes flashing with hunger, and he was overcome with the need to kiss her. Kiss her now. Lowering his head, he captured her lush lips as fireworks exploded behind his eyes and his heart pounded wildly against his ribs.

* * *

DEE MELTED into his long lean body; her hands splayed on his taut back as they kissed. Jaxon's lips were magic, so soft and gentle, yet firm and unrelenting. Like he burned to kiss her as much as she burned to kiss him. She let out a small moan as she parted her lips and let his tongue explore and tangle with hers. With her invitation to deepen the embrace, he slid a hand up the line of neck to the nape as he gripped her hip with the other, his hold on her firm yet gentle. Running her hands over his sides, she could feel the ripple of his back muscles, making her want to explore every ridge and contour of what she was certain was a magnificent body underneath that sweater. Sliding her hands around and up his chest to hook around his neck, he surprised her by lifting her and making a little squeak escape her throat. He smiled against her lips as he settled her on the island, his hard, tight body between her thighs as he continued to kiss her hungrily. Dee wasn't sure how long they made out, time no longer relevant, each seeming to never get enough. Reluctantly, he pulled his lips from hers, hovering only an inch from her mouth as they breathed the same air, hot and heavy. Dee, now completely drunk with lust, met his desire laden gaze, as he reached up and smoothed his thumb over her kiss bitten bottom lip.

"What are you doing to me, Ms. Jones?" he whispered huskily, his breaths coming in short and staccato.

"I should ask you the same question, Cowboy." she rasped, her ample chest heaving and pressing into his with each strained breath. "I've never felt like this before. Like I need to kiss you…"

"Now." he finished her sentence, his blue eyes flashing with desire.

She nodded, and reached into his hair, loving how soft it felt between her fingers as she tugged his mouth back to hers, kissing him sensually and making a low rumble reverberate from deep in his chest. He pulled back again, taking in another deep breath and letting it out slowly.

"If we don't stop, I can't guarantee I'm going to continue to be a gentleman," he confessed, meeting her wanton gaze.

Dee smiled, flashing him her dimpled smile as she asked playfully, "That was you kissing like a gentleman?"

A grin tugged at his lips, and Jaxon let out a deep, rich laugh, wrapping his strong arms around her in a hug. Dee laughed too, burying her face in his hard chest, his woodsy smell so deliciously inviting and quickly becoming addictive. He kissed her forehead and gently lifted her off the counter, holding her waist as she steadied herself on her now wobbly knees.

"I think I need to invite you over for dinner more often." She teased, letting out a long exhale as she touched her cheeks that were flushed hot from their make-out session

"You know where to find me," he replied with a flirty smile, his eyes still lustful and teeming with desire.

"I do." She answered, opening the cupboard and reaching for two plates. Grabbing a serving spoon, she glanced at the delicious-looking pasta that was now cold and laughed, shaking her head. "I need to warm up the pasta."

Jaxon laughed too as he took a seat at the island and watched her turn on the burner again and warm their dinner. Once their pasta was warmed and plated, they sat together side by side at the island, digging in.

"This is really delicious, Dee." he complimented, meeting her gaze and flashing her his endearing smile. "Just spicy enough."

She laughed and took a bite too, nodding in approval. Swallowing, a curious thought crossed her mind, and she turned to him with a question. "Were you aware that I lived down the hall from you?"

"Honestly, I had no idea, but I'm glad you do," he replied, reaching for her hand. He laced his fingers with hers and she glanced down, liking the way they fit together. He met her gaze, his eyes questioning. "Is it going to be weird now that we know we're neighbors? We kind of made out like two horny teenagers on your kitchen island?" he questioned, his face blooming into a blush with his words.

He's so cute. Dee tilted her head slightly, leaning into a dramatic pause as she read the apprehension. "Doesn't have to be weird unless we make it weird." She answered, her lips lifting into a coquettish grin as she added. "In fact, after dinner, if you wanted to kiss me again, like that, I'm game."

Jaxon let out a deep rich laugh that made Dee's insides tingle and glanced down at their intertwined hands. "Seriously, though, can I take you out on a date this weekend?" he asked, meeting her with a hopeful gaze. "I would like to get to know you more."

She leaned in, brushed his lips with a chaste kiss and met his eyes as she replied, "I thought you'd never ask."

JAXON COULDN'T GET the firework of a woman, Ms. Devine Jones, out of his mind. Last night was so much more than he expected. When she invited him over for dinner, he knew there was a mutual attraction there, but when they kissed, that attraction became combustible. It was almost unexplainable to him. He had never felt that kind of chemistry before with anyone. Ever. After getting their make-out session on her kitchen island under control, they ate dinner together, enjoying an evening of amazing conversation and endless laughter. She was so inquisitive, wanting to know about him growing up in Primrose, about his family and his brothers. She was genuinely interested in his upcoming construction projects and the second phase of the town-home/condo development on the west end of town. She asked questions about him personally and seemed to truly listen and take in his answers, cataloguing each detail he shared. It seemed like a lifetime since anyone had shown him that much interest and the warmth it gave him was addictive.

During their evening together, Dee was so open and forthcoming, talking about her mother and how close they were. She expressed with such excitement her love for acting and musicals and he helped her unpack the last boxes and fill her bookshelf. As they went through the various books and scripts from previous productions, she had been a part of; she shared stories about each one and why they were so special to her. The way she talked with so much joy and unbridled passion was contagious that by the time he left her condo with one last lingering kiss, he was sure an unending smile was permanently painted on his face. Even today, just the memory of last night, had him grinning like the Cheshire Cat.

"Good morning, J." his business partner Davis Baxter greeted as he entered his open office door and took a seat in the chair across from him. Whenever they were both in the office, they would enjoy their morning coffee together and go over the progress on current projects as well as anything upcoming. With a coffee cup in one hand and a pink bakery box in the other, he set the box on his desk. Jaxon glanced into the box and groaned in approval, his tongue immediately darting out to lick his lips.

"Hiring you, Davis, may be the best decision I've ever made. I get all the perks," he said, lifting out a freshly baked blueberry muffin and taking a generous bite, then nodding in approval as he chewed.

"Now I know why you hired me," he guffawed as he plucked a muffin from the box for himself and held it out in front of him. "Try being married to a pastry chef. Baked goods morning, noon, and night." Davis laughed with a pat of his belly before he too took a big bite of the break-fast treat.

Jaxon grinned at his business partner and friend. All joking aside, hiring Davis Baxter was one of the best busi-ness decisions he had ever made. Having joined him in business a year ago, Davis was ex-military, smart, savvy, highly educated and his expertise as a mechanical engi-neer was invaluable to their business. He wasn't sure if he could have completed phase one of the East End Project without him and, after completion, he officially made him a partner in his business. Now, Davis had become one of closest friends and confidantes.

"So, what did you do last night after we shut down the construction site?" Davis asked. "Glad we shut down early, as that rain and snow came out of nowhere."

Jaxon smiled wide, thinking about rescuing Dee from the unexpected turn in weather and how they huddled in his truck watching the rain transform to snow. "I had dinner with my neighbor," he replied simply, tilting his chair back as he grinned from ear to ear.

A smile tugged at Davis's lips as he asked, "Neighbor? Was this neighbor, by chance, a beautiful woman?"

"Yes, the new drama teacher at Primrose High." he replied, taking another bite of the muffin in his hand.

"You had dinner with Dee Jones?" Davis asked, sitting up straighter, his grin turning into a full out smile.

"You know, Dee?" Jaxon asked, almost choking on his bite as he leaned forward, set down the muffin, and rested his elbows on his desk.

"Yeah, she helped my brother-in-law, Rami's band with their social media and pretty much helped them breakthrough in the business. She's best friends with my sister-in-law, Savanah." he replied. "And I've met her several times. She's a lot of fun to be around."

"That she is." Jaxon added, his smile wide. "I rescued her from the storm when she was on her way home last night and she invited me over for dinner to thank me," he explained, his gaze drifting off in thought. "I asked her out on a date for this Saturday."

"You waste no time, my friend," Davis replied. "Do you know where you're going to take her?"

"Not sure yet, but it needs to be special," he said, with a laugh and shaking his head. "I'm so out of practice, man. I have no idea where to begin."

Davis leaned back, rubbing his chin as he thought, then answered, "Knowing what I know about Dee, she'll appreciate whatever you plan, but my advice is to do something you enjoy with her. It will help her to get to know you better, and that is never a bad thing."

Jaxon nodded his head in agreement. *That's good advice.* A few ideas popped into his head and he settled on one that had him written all over it. *I know exactly where I'm going to take her.*

* * *

CURLED UP IN A COZY BLANKET, Dee nursed her glass of wine as she gazed out over the expansive front lawn of her best friend Savanah's beautiful character home. She loved this property, which was large and surprisingly private and quiet for a house on the Main Street of Primrose. It was probably the huge, towering oak trees that surrounded the property that acted like a sound barrier and protected it from too many prying eyes. As the wife of Ramiro Perez, the lead singer of Prairie Sound, a popular indie rock band, this property was seemingly modest for a rock star, but it fulfilled their mutual desire for a simple, quiet small-town life in Primrose. Plus, the house and property oozed character and charm, which suited both Rami and Savanah to perfection.

Savanah pushed through the front door, the storm door slamming behind her as she held a glass of wine in one hand, and balanced a platter of crackers, cheese, and grapes in the other. She set down the tray and Dee immediately set down her wineglass and swooped in to pick up a cracker, a piece of brie, and a bunch of grapes. She bit into the cracker and cheese and moaned out her approval. "You make a mean cheese platter, my friend," he mumbled through her bite, before popping a grape into her mouth.

Savanah laughed sardonically. "That's because that's all I can make. Thank goodness Rami can cook, otherwise we would both starve."

"There's always the Eazy or Lings." Dee reassured with a laugh as she paused, grape halfway to her mouth, her eyes brightening. "What I wouldn't give for Lings beef and broccoli right now!"

Savanah nodded in agreement and looked down at her housecoat and pjs as she pulled her blanket over her shoulders and frowned. "That means we would have to abandon the PJ's."

Dee wrapped her blanket tighter around her body. "Not a chance," she replied, making Savanah giggle in agreement.

When Rami started touring with his band, a few years back and would be gone for weeks at a time, Dee and Savanah started a Friday night pajama party tradition, which they continued even after Savanah and Rami had married and moved to Primrose. When Rami wasn't home on a Friday, Dee was there with her best friend to keep her company. It was a time she cherished with her oldest and dearest friend.

"Speaking of dinner. I had someone over for dinner on Wednesday." she informed, wiggling her brows at her best friend. "A certain gentleman caller." She added in a very believable British accent.

"Ooh, do tell, fair lady," Savanah replied, attempting to sound regal.

"A Mr. Jaxon Isley." Dee replied instinctively, biting her bottom lip at the thought of the impossibly handsome man. "He lives just down the hall from me and rescued me from the strange snow squall the other day."

"That was weird." Savanah nodded, as she sat up and asked. "So, like the Jaxon Isley that owns Isley Construction?"

"That's the one! To thank him for saving me from a freezing and wet walk home, I invited him to dinner, and we ended up cooking together then making out on my kitchen island." She confessed, lifting her glass to take a quick sip of her wine and wait for her friend's inevitable reaction.

"You had sex on your kitchen island?" Savanah asked, her eyes wide as a smile lifted her lips.

"No, but let me tell you, I'm not sure I would have stopped it if he took it there." Dee confessed, letting out a low whistle. "We full-out kissed, though. Like breathless, mind-bending kissing."

"Ooh, that's the best kind of kissing." Savanah mused, her cheeks flushing pink.

"Yeah!" Dee added. "He has this sexy country boy thing going, and Lord have mercy he can kiss. Hands down the best kiss of my life."

Savanah smiled at her bestie and picked up her wine glass, holding it up between them. "I propose a toast." Dee gave her a wide smile as she lifted her glass. "To hot kisses on kitchen counters." Savanah declared, raising her glass with a mischievous twinkle in her eyes. "And even hotter sex."

Both girls giggled, clinked their glasses, and took a drink. *Hot sex with Jaxon. Now that's a thought.* Dee brought fingertips to her lips at the memory of their scorching kiss. *Am I ready for that?* Honestly, she didn't know. But what she did know is that when they were together, the need to touch him was tangible and she wanted so much more.

CHAPTER 4

*D*ee had changed her outfit at least four times in the past 15 minutes. *Why am I so nervous about this date?* She wasn't one to get nervous or worked up over a guy. She had always been a confident woman and could hold her own with anyone, but for some reason, her far too handsome neighbour had her somewhat flustered. He was just so quiet and laid back and exuded this "I don't know how hot I am" sex appeal. She had never met anyone quite like him, and something about that intrigued her. His humility was completely refreshing and unquestionably sexy.

Internally scolding herself for not asking Jaxon what to expect tonight, she settled on a red wrap jumpsuit that extenuated her petite curvaceous body and a pair of high heel boots that were sure to give her five-foot five frame a little more height. Giving herself a final once over, she declared, "I'm ready." *But am I?* The last time they were together, they went from zero to sixty on the steam meter, but then they slowed down and got to know each other more. With a nod and a determined glare at herself in the mirror, she made the decision that she needed to focus on the latter part of their last encounter and not think about how sinfully good he kissed. Just the thought of it made her body ignite with desire. Dee shook her head, to try to erase the thoughts and took a deep steadying breath. *Be cool, be breezy. Keep your libido in check. You are a strong, independent woman who has control over her mind and body.* A knock sounded at the door, and she raised her chin at her reflection in the mirror as she repeated her mantra one more time before heading to the door to greet Jaxon. Opening the door, Jaxon stood, leaning casually against the door frame, dressed in a white t-shirt, dark wash jeans and a black leather jacket looking like sex on a stick. *Meow! Screw the mantra.*

"Well, hello there, Cowboy." she rasped out sexily. One corner of his mouth curled up into a smirk as his far to perfect blue eyes twinkled with approval at her greeting.

That was something she had already figured out about Jaxon during their evening together. He was an easy man to read. What you saw was what he was. A truly authentic man, who radiated warmth when he smiled. From her past dating experiences, authenticity was a rarity and Dee had encountered more than her share of "the cover not being what was in the book".

"Hi." he said huskily. "You..." he paused, taking in the fiery red ensemble with complete admiration. Dee was aware she looked like a million bucks in it, but as Jaxon raised his gaze to meet hers and breathed out. "You're beautiful." Dee confirmed she was in trouble. A heap of trouble in the form of a six-foot two country boy.

Butterflies, flocks of birds and fireworks all took off in her belly with his sweet and simple compliment and she had to mentally control her instinct to melt like a puddle on the floor. She looked down at her outfit and back to his gorgeous blue eyes, so full of warmth and sincerity as she replied. "Thank you. You look…" *Hot, smoking, edible!* Her inner voice was having a field day with possible adjectives. "You look handsome." She said. *That was appropriate. High five outer voice.*

Jaxon smoothed his hand down the edge of his jacket and smiled at her as he asked, "Are you ready to go?"

Grabbing her purse, she reached into the closet, pulled out her favorite leather jacket, and slid it on before she replied, "Now I am."

He grinned as she locked her door and put his hand out to her in offering. Dee took it, feeling the now familiar warmth of his touch surge through her as they made their way to the elevator together.

Pulling into the parking lot of what appeared to be a sporting goods store, Dee took one look at the unassuming building and turned to Jaxon, squinting her eyes at him, a smile tugging at her lips. "Doing a little personal shopping before our date. Need a jersey or a jockstrap?"

Jaxon laughed, his voice rich and deep as he undid his seatbelt and turned to her to reply, "This is a place my father used to take me when I was a teen. This place has batting cages at the back of the building. I was a professional baseball player for 12 years and, well, I wanted to bring you to a place that's special to me."

Dee smiled and touched his hand resting on the seat

between them. "I love it, J. Seriously, this is going to be fun," she said, leaning in and planting a chaste kiss on his lips before she opened her door and slid out of his truck. Turning to face him, she said, "I can't wait to see those pro moves."

Jaxon grinned, taking a beat to relish the lingering tingle of her quick kiss, before exiting the cab and meeting Dee at the front door of the store. He held the door for her and once both had entered; he took her hand, threading his fingers with hers.

"Jaxon, my man! How are ya?" a tall, handsome middle-aged man, with dark skin, obsidian eyes, and shortcut tightly curled salt sprinkled hair greeted from behind the counter as they approached.

"Fantastic, Dex and you?" Jaxon replied, clapping hands with him and giving him a companionable fist pump.

"Can't complain, can't complain…" Dex answered, his kind gaze slowly drifting over to Dee. Now, who do we have here?"

"Dex, this is Devine Jones." he said, turning his eyes to her with sweet affection.

Dex hesitated as a look of nostalgia washed over his face. He cleared his throat and smiled, as he asked, "Devine, did you say? That's a unique name. Are you by chance named after the famous actress Loretta Devine?"

"I am." Dee brightened as she met his dark, expressive eyes. "Do you know *Dream Girls*?"

"Do I know *Dream Girls*?" Dex echoed back, letting out a low whistle. "I played Curtis Taylor Jr. in a production in the 90s."

"I had no idea you were a thespian." Jaxon commented to his longtime friend.

"What can I say? I'm a man of many interests and talents," he replied with a grin before he turned his warm gaze back to Dee and he offered his hand to her in greeting. "I'm Dexter Geoffrey the Third. But please call me Dex."

"Fancy name." She added with a grin of her own. "Pleasure to meet you, Dex. I'm a former stage actress myself, but now I teach drama at Primrose High School."

"Dee is directing a production of *Singin' in the Rain* which will hit the stage this June." Jaxon added, with pride in his voice.

"Ahh! A Gene Kelly classic!" Dex exclaimed. "Do you think you could reserve a ticket for me? I still love a good musical."

"Absolutely." she answered, cocking a curious brow at him. "Will you need two? Perhaps take a date with you?"

He let out a huge guffaw. "It seems my dating days are over. Alas, I have already met the love of my life and she rejected me." he added with his hand resting over his heart.

Although Dex was trying to answer lightly, Jaxon could see a glimmer of pain behind his eyes, and he could tell Dee saw it too as she replied brightly. "Consider one ticket reserved for the handsome Dexter Geoffrey the Third!" then flashed him a playful wink

Dex laughed deeply as he turned his gaze to Jaxon. "Beautiful, smart, and sassy. I like this girl! Jaxon, you hold tight to her!"

Jaxon flashed her a smile and pulled Dee to his side,

wrapping a claiming arm around her shoulders. Dee glanced up at him, her midnight eyes twinkling with pure mirth and Jaxon smiled so wide his cheeks hurt. Dee exuded boundless confidence and sharp wit, and he found her ability to hold her own in any scenario wildly attractive.

Jaxon paid for an hour in the batting cages and led Dee through a door at the back of the building where the cages were set up. The sound of the rattling engine of the ball machine, baseballs hitting the chain-link fence, and the echoing sound of laughter carried through the expansive room. A dad with his teenage son, and a group of rowdy twenty something guys in and surrounding their cages, were the only other patrons there. The click of Dee's high heel boots on the concrete floor made them all stop and turn as he and Dee strode by, claiming the cage in the far corner. An appreciative whistle sounded from behind them, which Jaxon suspected came from the group of young men. Dee, completely unphased, glanced up at Jaxon as they reached their cage, bestowed on him her sexy dimpled smile, and slipped her arm around his waist curling her fingers around him as she asked, "Can you show me how it's done?"

"Of course," he replied as she let go of him and Jaxon slid out of his jacket. Dee followed suit as he grabbed a helmet, before leaning down and hovering just over her mouth. She gazed up at him through her long lashes and hooking her fingers into the loops of his jeans, went on her tiptoes and bridged the distance, kissing him softly and sensually. Releasing their kiss, she reached up, affectionately wiping the hint of lipstick that transferred to his lips before he got into the cage. Cuing up the ball machine, he lifted the aluminum bat and took his stance. The first ball shot out of the machine and Jaxon connected with it expertly. The next five were just the same, the ping of his bat echoing through the large space and drawing the attention of the other patrons. His round done, he turned to Dee, who stood there slack jawed as a smile slowly curled on her sweet lips.

"Show off!" she exclaimed, her mouth turning into a full out smile.

He exited the cage, feeling the familiar high he got whenever he came here. He loved baseball, the weight of the bat in his hand, and sometimes he missed his Minor League days. He strode over to Dee, removed the helmet, and handed it to her. "Are you ready to get your bat on, Ms. Jones?"

"Am I ready? I was born ready!" she exclaimed with pure excitement and enthusiasm as she set the helmet on her head and he reached out and adjusted the strap around her chin, tucking a few stray braids inside the helmet.

"Have you ever played baseball before?" he asked, meeting her gaze.

"Nope. But can you show me how to swing before that machine over there starts pitching to me?" she asked, gesturing over to the ball machine.

Jaxon nodded, handed her the bat, and positioned himself at her back. He reached around her body to settle his hands on hers as they gripped the bat. Dee wiggled her bottom against his groin and glanced over her shoulder, giving him a sexy grin. A low growly rumble reverberated from his chest and she did it again, letting out a raspy laugh. That sexy lilt of her voice made him very aware of her control over his body and how she could so easily unravel him. Positioning her hands on the bat, he took her through a few practice swings and when he thought she was ready; he let go, letting her do it on her own. "That's it. Keep your head up and eye on the ball and you'll connect with it."

"Okay, I got it!" she replied eagerly as she entered the cage.

She took her stance as he showed her, and the first ball flew past her, hitting the chain-link fence as she swung just a hair too late.

"That's alright. Keep your eye on the ball and swing straight through. You almost had that first one." He encouraged, clapping his hands.

The next ball launched, and she swung, connecting the aluminum bat, which made the familiar ping. Dee beamed but kept her stance, connecting three more times out of the next four finishing her round.

Jaxon was flabbergasted and teeming with pride. He had never seen anything like it. First time in the cage, never played ball and connected on four out of the six. He simply laughed as before him, was this gorgeous woman, dressed like a hot as hell red vixen in high heels, a baseball helmet on her head cheering and shaking her hips in a victory happy dance. The commotion she created drew the attention of the other patrons and everyone stopped what they were doing to look her way, with huge smiles on their faces. Coming out of the cage, she took the helmet off, shook out her braids, and beamed up at Jaxon, her face glowing with pure joy and mirth. One of the twenty something guys shouted across the room. "Great job!"

Dee glanced at him and, in only the way she could, took a flourishing bow before her attention returned to Jaxon's.

"You are so crazy sexy right now," he said, a look of awe and wonder on his face.

She reached up, hooked her arms around his neck and jumped into his arms, wrapping her legs around his waist. His breath caught in surprise as her eyes shimmered and she whispered, "Thank you for teaching me."

"My pleasure." He whispered back and captured her lips with his in a raw, needy kiss.

Hoots and hollers sounded from their twenty something friends and Dee broke their kiss, throwing her head back in a raspy laugh, making Jaxon laugh as well. Setting her down, he intertwined his hands with hers as he asked, "How about we get out of here and grab some dinner?"

"Yes! I am starving!" she exclaimed as she released his hands and grabbed her jacket, putting it on with him following suit. They walked out hand in hand, both on a high from not only the batting practice, but from each other.

* * *

SITTING beside Jaxon in a booth at a well-known steakhouse, the ambiance dimly lit and intimate, Dee couldn't believe how much she liked this guy. He was so laid back and calm and just being in his presence filled her with so much peace. She self-admittedly was tightly wound up on a good day, so his quiet contrast to her loud boldness was so refreshing. Dee tended to end up with guys just like her. Bold, loud, and confident. Although Jaxon came across as confident, it was a quiet confidence, and his humbleness was incredibly attractive to her. There was nothing pretentious or cocky about Jaxon Isley.

"Tell me about your professional baseball career." She urged with curiosity. "You must have travelled a lot and seen some fantastic cities."

"I did, and it was a lot of fun. I loved the game so much and every chance I had to play, I was happy. When you travel with your team, you become close friends too, so the camaraderie is a huge part of what I loved about playing. I'm still good friends with many of my teammates.

"That's not unlike when you're part of a cast for a production. You spend so much time together you start to feel like a family." she compared; fondness reflected in her gaze.

"You do," he agreed, before giving her a sweet smile. "That's a good way to describe it."

"Do you miss it?" Dee asked, her brows drawing together with the question.

"Very much, but it was time to move on." He replied, meeting her gaze with resolution. "Looking back now, I don't regret leaving the game when I did."

A contemplative silence fell on the pair with his confession, and Dee could see there was more to the story than he was sharing. Choosing not to press further, she leaned into him, resting her hand on his thigh as she started flirtatiously. "So, J, I've been wondering about something since I met you." His eyes grew hooded with her touch. "What's a handsome guy like you doing single? I mean, from where I'm sitting, you, Jaxon, are the entire package."

Jaxon let out a low chuckle at her question, as his brows drew together and his expression morphed to seriousness. A flash of pain swept across his face as he reached for his wine, took a sip, then cleared his throat nervously, setting it back down on the table.

Dee met his gaze, his blue eyes reflecting past sadness, and she took his hand, lacing her fingers with his. "Did I hit a sore spot?" she asked, giving his hand a supportive squeeze. "You don't have to answer if you don't want to."

"No, it's okay. It's a valid question and one you have every right to ask. I just have never had to share my story on a date before and well I…I don't want you to see it as a red flag."

Dee straightened her back slightly, bracing herself for something. She didn't know what. Hand still tethered to his, her eyes encouraging him to open to her.

"I'm divorced." He answered, searching her eyes for what she assumed was apprehension. *Sorry Cowboy, that doesn't faze me.* Taking in her lack of reaction to this personal information, he cleared his throat again, now fueled to continue. "I was with my ex for eight years and married for five years."

"Is she from Primrose?" Dee asked curiously, genuinely wanting to know more about this insane woman that would give up such a good man.

"No, she was originally from New York City but

moved to the Toronto area after we split up," he replied. "I honestly don't know exactly where she is these days. We've been divorced for a long time."

Dee shook her head and let out a long breath as she asked. "Was it a bad breakup?"

"You could say that. She ended up cheating on me with one of my teammates that made it to the Majors before I did and shortly after we divorced, got engaged to him," he shared. "I don't know if they actually got married, as once I found out about their relationship behind my back, I cut all ties with him. He was one of my best friends too, so I not only lost my wife, but was betrayed by a friend."

Dee flinched and shook her head, then let out a puff of air as his gaze rose to meet hers. Her eyes searched his blue depths and her heart ached, thinking about how hurt he must have been. Eyes locked on his, she reached out and touched his cheek affectionately as she said, "She didn't deserve someone as special as you. Jaxon, you're a truly amazing man."

With her words lingering between them, she leaned in and brushed her lips tenderly to his. He leaned into the kiss and something beautiful and pure passed between them. He seemed to let go of a breath he had been holding and she could feel his body relax next to her.

Breaking their kiss, he looked into her eyes and confessed, his voice low and deep. "I really like you, Dee."

"I like you too, J." she replied with a sweet smile. "Very much."

Jaxon smiled sweetly, his eyes following her gentle caress of her fingertips up and down his arm. Dee could literally see him trying to process his thoughts and formulate the words as he said. "I need to be totally honest with you that this thing that's happening between us is all going kind of fast for me..." he started, making her pause her caress and look up, meeting his gaze. "...but I don't want to slow it down, Dee." he added, putting it all out there. "I don't want this evening with you to end."

"It doesn't have to." She rasped out, hopefulness in her tone as she met his gaze, desire in their depths. "I think you and I both want the same thing, don't we?"

"I think we do." He replied, tucking a braid behind her ear as he searched her eyes, and he drew in a deep inhale as he continued. "I need you to know I didn't go into this date with expectations." he clarified. "But I'm not going to lie to you and say I haven't thought about spending the night with you since that incredible kiss in your kitchen."

"I've thought about it too," she confessed, looking down at their hands laced together before her eyes drifted slowly back to Jaxon's. "So, I guess here we are. Two consenting adults, wildly attracted to each other, wanting to deepen our connection."

"Looks like that's where we are," he agreed, raising her hand to his and planting a gentle kiss on it, just before he flagged down their waiter to bring them the check.

PULLING into the parking lot of their condo building, the air in the cab of Jaxon's truck was charged with sexual tension. Dee glanced over to Jaxon, whose hand had taken on a vibrating tremor despite his cool as a cucumber persona he was attempting to convey. He undid his seatbelt, and she followed suit, both meeting each other's gaze expectantly when they were no longer buckled. It took everything in her not to pull him closer and take what she wanted right there in the parking lot. But before her libido did something impulsive, Jaxon exited his truck, and she watched him come around to her side, opening her door for her. She smiled at the gentlemanly gesture, feeling like it was a foreshadow of what would happen tonight. How he would take care of her. Taking her hand, he helped her out of the tall truck and closed the door behind her. Intertwining his fingers with hers, they walked quietly together into the condo building and onto the elevator, their eyes locked on each other's as the rapidly rising tension between them wound tight like a coil ready to break. When they got to their floor, both stopped at the halfway point between their apartments and looked at each other in question.

"My place or yours?" Jaxon asked, glancing down at her.

"Mine tonight, yours next time." She answered, and she could see his eyes darken with desire at her confident expectation. *There will definitely be a next time.*

Unlocking her door, she walked into her condo, Jaxon following closely behind her. As soon as she locked the door, Jaxon's hands were on her hips, his long, lean body pressed against her back as his lips found the side of her neck.

"J," Dee breathed out, as she turned in his arms to face him, a look of pure lust reflecting at her. A wave of desire surged through her body as he pressed her into the door and crushed his lips to hers, raw and hungry. He kissed her with abandon, as she slipped his jacket off his shoulders, dropping it to the floor, and he did the same to her before pressing her again into the hard wooden door. Her body burned, red hot heat igniting like a wildfire as he lifted her, his large hands cupping her behind. She panted breathless against his lips. "Bedroom."

Jaxon turned, his eyes blazing with heat as he carried her past the main living area, down the short hall to the master bedroom at the end. Setting her down on her feet, he reached over his head, pulling off his T-shirt, revealing his magnificent upper body beneath. Dee drank him in, admiring all his lean, sinewy muscles. Before she could continue her appreciative perusal, he leaned in, capturing her lips again in a scorching kiss as her hands started to explore the taut groves and ridges of his torso. Dee broke their passionate kiss, her eyes catching on the beautiful ink on his arm. What looked like the beginnings of a sleeve of tattoos, intricately woven together, both surprised and delighted her. She traced a line of birds that trailed up his arm towards a detailed compass on his shoulder, with roses blooming behind it. She glanced up at him, meeting his wanton gaze as he reached for the sash in her jumpsuit and started to untie it. Dee turned around, showing him where the zipper was, and he slid it down slowly, revealing her smooth dark skin as his fingertips caressed with each tug and pull. She quivered from the tender touch as he slipped one shoulder down, then the other and she took over, sliding the remainder of the jumpsuit over her curvaceous hips and behind. Standing there in only a red lace bra with matching thong and her killer high heel boots, she stepped out of her clothes and glanced up, meeting his lustful gaze.

Jaxon's eyes roamed hungrily over every amble curve of her body as he took her in, and his gaze lifted to hers. "You are so beautiful, Dee." he said softly with such reverence her breath caught. No one had ever looked at her like this or talked to her that way. Like he was complimenting not only her outer beauty but the beauty within. Something inside of Dee shifted in that moment. She wasn't sure what it was, nor did she have time to analyze her feelings right now. All she knew for certain is she wanted this man, needed to kiss him again and to feel those strong, calloused hands on her body. Before she could pull him into another kiss, much to her dismay Jaxon dropped to his knees in front of her, slowly sliding the zipper of one boot down, then the other caressing her calf, ankle, and foot as he helped her out of them. The gesture was sweet, caring, and so completely erotic. Her head spun. All she could do was watch and revel in the attention he was giving her with each small touch as she pooled with desire.

JAXON WAS ON FIRE, his entire body electric as he knelt before her. Looking up and meeting her lust drunk gaze, he paused for a moment, wanting to worship at the feet of Ms. Devine Jones. This woman before him was a goddess, and he needed her to know how much he wanted her. Jaxon rose to his feet and swooped her up in his arms, making her croon with appreciation. Laying her out in the middle of the bed, he took a self-indulgent moment to take in her beauty. Her ebony skin was so flawlessly smooth, and her supple, lush curves dipped and swelled into a perfect hourglass figure. Dee was beyond stunning and undoubtedly the most beautiful woman he had ever laid eyes on.

Undressing himself, he slipped off his shoes and socks, then reached for his belt, unfastening it, and pulling it out, tossing it to the floor with the rest of their discarded clothes. Unbuttoning his jeans, he unzipped them and slid them down his long legs, adding them to the pile. Standing before her in just his black boxer briefs, she sat up, met his eyes, not leaving them as she reached behind her back and unfastened her bra, slipping it off and tossing it to the floor. His breath hitched at the sight of her exquisite body and pert breasts beckoning him. She lay back down, the carnal lust in her eyes drawing him forward. Climbing onto the bed, he covered her with the heat of his body, caging her in, all her soft curves pressed to his hard chest as he nestled between her legs. They stared into each other's eyes, gazes intense with desire, the combustible heat between them sweltering as he shared, his voice husky with need. "I want to be inside you, Dee, but before I do, I need to savor you."

Jaxon kissed her passionately before his lips roamed and he blazed a trail of licks, kisses, and nips, down her neck, over her collarbone and in between her breasts before he raised his head giving her a sexy grin and he took a pebbled peak into his mouth sucking it deep. She moaned out in pleasure as he lavished one breast then the other, causing her to cry out his name and gasp with pleasure. Once he had his fill, he continued his path of kisses down her stomach, heading south. Reaching her apex, he kissed the wet with arousal juncture of her legs and hooked his fingers in the sides of her thong. She lifted her body to help him as he slid them down her legs, then off, tossing them to the side. Spreading her legs wide, he salivated as he took in her glistening center. *So pretty.* Kissing her thighs, running his scruff over the sensitive skin, on one leg then the other, he brought his mouth so excruciatingly close to where she ached for him to touch and inhaled the sweet scent of her arousal.

"Jaxon, please." She begged as she groaned at his taunting.

With her plea, he slid his tongue up the seam of her with one long languid stroke and circled where she pulsed with need. Dee gasped with pleasure as he lapped at her sensitive folds, savoring the sweet nectar of her desire. The way she responded to each lick, flick, and tease spurred him to continue his ravenous torture of her swollen with desire core. He had always enjoyed going down on a woman, giving more than he took, but with Dee, her sheer unbridled response to his worshiping tongue fueled his own desire and he could already feel the slow burn building at the base of his spine. Unapologetically, Dee rocked into mouth, bowed, and arched as he expertly brought her over the edge, her sweet arousal flooding his tongue, her body trembling beautifully against his mouth. Her chest heaving with each breath, he raised himself off the bed and eased off his underwear. Her dark eyes met his as her gaze roamed down his body, settling on his long hard length, every smooth inch poised and ready to give her pleasure. Lips curling into a smile, she reached for her nightstand, slid open the top drawer, reached inside and produced a foil packet.

"You're full of surprises, Ms. Jones," he said with a grin as he crawled up her body, his knees brushing her behind. She handed him the condom and watched as he made short work of sheathing himself, then climbed the rest of the way over her, his hard ridge nestled between her aching folds. "Tell me what you like and what feels good, okay?"

She nodded, her dark eyes hazy with desire as he lifted, positioned himself at her entrance and sank in slowly, relishing the way her body opened and hugged his length. As he filled her, she moaned in approval as her slick heat tightened and pulsed around him. His brows pinched together, and he had to still for a moment, the feel of her body too mind-bendingly hot, tight and perfect.

"Are you okay?" she rasped, breathless.

"Yes, you just feel so damn good," he managed roughly in reply as his eyes locked on hers.

Dee grinned naughtily at his response and rocked her hips up, taking him deeper. He groaned as he pulled back and rocked into her again, the exquisite friction of her tight heat drawing him in. Capturing her lips in a bruising kiss, their bodies moved together in tandem, her meeting him with each press and grind of his hips. Their sensual sounds filled the room, and he was consumed by the sheer pleasure of their connection. His release building, Dee let out a sexy purr of pleasure beneath him, and from the pulsing grip of her body, he could tell she was getting close. Sweat skimming their bodies, he brought her hands over her head, his hands intertwined with hers as he took the peak of a breast in his mouth and sucked it in deep, making her moan loudly, as he thrust harder, deeper, faster chasing her climax as well as his own. She let out a throaty gasp as her body gripped him like a vice and she crashed, wave after wave of pleasure rippling through her, causing his own earth-shattering release to slam into him. He continued to move, wanting to feel every ripple and pulse until they both were left trembling with aftershocks.

"Are you okay?" he asked, his hands on either side of her head, their bodies flush and hot skin slick.

She threaded her fingers through his hair, tugging as her lush mouth curled into a satiated smile and she countered in question. "Do you even have to ask?"

Jaxon laughed, her joining as he planted a tender kiss to her lips. Knowing he was crushing her, he rolled to the side and off the bed to dispose of the condom and when he returned, Dee was still laying there gorgeously naked on top of the covers. *This woman.* Dee rolled onto her side, pinned him with her midnight gaze and crooked a finger at him, beckoning him to join her in bed. Like a moth to a flame, he complied, sliding in next to her and pulling her flush with his long lean, taut body, his hand running over her behind and lifting her leg to curl around his. Dee tenderly brushed the hair from his forehead, feathering fingers through his hair as she met his gaze with so much affection it made his heart swell. Something profound passed between them, a deep sense of knowing that was hard to describe. All he knew for certain at that moment was that his life was about to change.

CHAPTER 5

*D*ee woke up the next morning feeling exquisitely sore, undeniably satiated, and completely intoxicated with lust as she thought about her passionate night with Jaxon. Grinning with satisfaction, she stretched her arms above her then realized she was alone in the bed. The place he had been sleeping was still warm, so she rolled over on the side and inhaled deeply, his woodsy scent still lingering on the pillow. Sighing blissfully as the memories of last night slowly came back. The way he took her, again and again, wringing every ounce of pleasure from her body and the way he looked at her with so much reverence and adoration. He had savored her as promised and took his time to figure out what she liked and how she liked it. As a self admittedly sex positive woman, Dee had her share of sexual experiences, but with Jaxon, it was different. She had never had anyone put her pleasure above their own. Jaxon was a giver, not a taker, and that made her want to flip the script to show him she could give as good as she took. With naughty thoughts stirring in her mind, her bedroom door slowly opened, and Jaxon walked into the room shirtless, looking completely edible, with all his lean, sinewy muscles on display. His jeans clung loosely on his narrow hips, and she couldn't help but take in the deep cut V flagging the trail of hair from his navel. *Happy trail indeed.*

Looking ruggedly handsome and sexily disheveled, Jaxon set a tray of what appeared to be coffee and toast on her end table. Dee sat up, pulled the covers over her breasts, and tucked her braids behind her ears. Jaxon offered her his endearing smile as he slid in beside her on the bed, his blue eyes dancing and his facial scruff longer than last night. She reached out and caressed her hand down his cheek, the rough texture making her think of how good it felt on her inner thighs.

"Good morning," he said coyly. "How did you sleep?"

"So good," she rasped, letting the covers fall from her bare breasts and raising her hands overhead to stretch her back.

"So did I." he replied, eyes darkening as he looked his fill, before pulling his appreciative gaze away to glance at the tray. "Are you hungry?"

"I am," she replied, pinning him with a vixen stare. "But not for food."

Jaxon's eyes shaded with desire, and a low growl rumbled from his chest as she climbed onto his lap and straddled his hips. His eyes roamed over her body with appreciation as his hands coasted over her cures. She rubbed her core over him as she ran her hands through his hair and gave it a tug, making him hiss with approval. "Last night, you made me the star of the show and although I love to be in the spotlight, as you know, I think you deserve a round of applause for giving me oh so many orgasms last night." She said, grinding her core hard over his impressive ridge. Gripping her hips, he dug his fingertips into the soft flesh, but she shook her head as she continued with a sexy smile, "You made last night all about me, so now it's all about you." With that, Dee climbed off him, popped the button of his jeans and he lifted his hips as she stripped him. Once Jaxon was naked, she crawled up his body, her eyes not leaving his. "You just lay back and let me take care of you."

Tucked between his legs, she raked her fingernails lightly over his chest and down his abdomen, making his engorged member twitch. With a wicked smile, she wrapped her fingers around his girth and stroked his hard length once, twice, three times, causing him to moan. Glancing up at him through her long lashes, she lowered her head and swirled her tongue around the crown before dipping it into the slit that already dripped with pleasure. His breath caught as she did this, and she grinned, knowing he was going to enjoy the sweet torture she was about to administer. "Do you like that?" she asked, her hand gripping the base of his pulsing shaft.

"Fuck, yes." he groaned dirtily, his eyes locked on hers.

"Good, then you're going to love this," she said, dipping her head, swirling her tongue and around the crown again before drawing him to the back of her throat.

"Fuck, Dee, sweet Jesus." he cursed, gripping the bed sheet for purchase. Jaxon threw his head back with pleasure, every taut muscle coiled tight as she sucked, licked, and stroked him, teasing and toying with his pleasure. His hips instinctively thrust up, hitting the back of her throat as she hummed with approval. Dee continued her merciless attention until he let out a long-pained groan, stilled and with one more swirl of her tongue spilled into her mouth. Dee drank in his arousal until he melted into the bed, body wrung out with pleasure.

With a satisfied grin, Dee crawled back over his body and straddled his hips, her eyes locked on his face, flushed and clouded with desire. He tried to speak, but she put her index finger over his mouth to stop him.

"No need to thank me, Cowboy." she said, both with unmeasurable confidence and a hint of mirth.

With her comment, Jaxon laughed, a full out body shaking laugh that made her join him and he said huskily. "I've never met anyone like you Dee. You're so unapologetically yourself and your confidence is sexy as hell."

Dee smiled, liking his astute observation, and leaned down devouring his lips in a slow sensual kiss. As their tongues tangled, she felt his body awaken again beneath her. Reaching over him into her bedside table drawer, she fished out a condom and presented it to him. "Get ready for the ride of your life, Cowboy." she said, cocking one eyebrow as she ripped open the condom package with her teeth. Sheathing his hard length, she rose to her knees, notched him at her entrance and sank her body down, eagerly welcoming him in. "You feel so perfect in me," she declared on a moan as she swiveled her hips with a delicious grind. His hands were everywhere, plucking, squeezing, gripping, relinquishing his control and letting her ride out her pleasure and his. Lost in sensation, Dee threw her head back and rested her palms behind her on his legs as she continued the sensual grind of her hips. The slight change in angle hit the coveted spot inside her as Jaxon reached between them and strummed his thumb against her aching center, causing her to detonate with an explosive release. He grabbed her hips, taking over and thrusting into her from beneath, drawing out her release and finding his own. Dee collapsed on top of him as the heat of her body against his made her shiver. Still connected, he wrapped his arms around her protectively as he brushed the braids from her face and kissed her forehead with tenderness. Dee met his affectionate gaze as she confessed, "I've never had it this good."

"Neither have I," he replied, only honesty and sincerity within his gaze. "I want to spend so much more time with you, Dee. I want so much more of this."

"I want that too," she replied, brushing the hair from his eyes, cocking a brow at him and giving him a mischievous grin. "I guess this means you want to date me."

"I think that means I want you to be my girlfriend, Dee. Are you okay with us putting a label on this?" he asked, gesturing between the two of them. "I know we just met but…"

Dee planted a chaste kiss on his lips, silencing his words. Pulling away she met his questioning gaze, so much sweet affection in their depths as she took his handsome face into her hands and kissed him again, this time deep and reverent before pulling away once more and replying, "Yes, I want to be your girlfriend, J."

His smile slowly widened, pure happiness on his face

as he rolled them over, making her laugh as he pinned her to the mattress.

* * *

THEY STAYED in bed all morning, kissing, touching, talking, and laughing. Jaxon's senses tingled with that nebulous feeling one gets when they really like someone, and just being in their presence makes you giddy. That sweet warm fuzzy feeling where one knows their heart has shown up to play.

"Tell me about your tattoo," she requested as she took a sip of her coffee and set it down on the nightstand.

Jaxon met her gaze and watched as she touched his ink, tracing the circle of the compass, her fingertips following the lines of the roses and the path of the birds. "The birds and compass represent finding your way home. If you notice, it's pointing southeast, which is where we are."

"I like that," she replied with a smile. "And the roses? I assume it's Primrose."

"Yes, but also for my mother. Her name is Rose."

"That's so sweet. When did you get it?" she asked curiously, meeting his soft gaze.

"When I returned to Manitoba after my divorce. I was pretty lost after that, like I didn't know where I belonged anymore. It was a very dark and difficult time for me. But when I came back here, I was reminded of what I love about this town. The people, the kindness, how everyone kind of looks out for each other. Primrose helped me start to heal." He shared wistfully before letting out an incredulous chuckle. "I don't think I've ever shared any of that with anyone."

Dee smoothed her hand down his inked arm and laced her fingers with his as she replied, "Thank you for sharing it with me."

He looked into her eyes, so full of gratitude and warmth. Dee's eyes were like an open book, each emotion so easy to read. She had an easy openness about her, and he appreciated that. "And you, I noticed some writing on your ribs, but I was a little too busy to read it," he said with a wink.

Dee nudged him playfully and laughed as she lifted her arm over her head to reveal the quote she had tattooed on her rib cage in handwriting.

"Here's what love is: a smoke made out of lover's sighs. When the smoke clears, love is a fire burning in your lover's eyes." – William Shakespeare

"It's from Romeo and Juliet." Dee explained. "I remember I was quite young the first time I read it. I was so enamored by the story. How two star-crossed lovers, from completely different worlds, wanted nothing more than to be together. It was so beautiful and tragic all in one." She shared passionately. "It's the kind of love I want to find. The kind of love that's so deep and burning within your soul that you can't live without them."

Jaxon ran his fingertips over the writing, so beautifully inked on her flawless skin. Lifting his gaze to meet her gorgeous midnight eyes, he tried to formulate a response to the beauty of the famous passage and the woman who adorned it. However, there didn't seem to be words poignant or special enough to say to this remarkable woman. A woman with so much ardor and depth, it astounded him. All he could manage was, "You are beautiful."

She lowered her arm, met his sincere gaze and leaned in brushing her lips to his in a sweet and tender kiss. Jaxon pulled her closer, already knowing he would never get enough of her as their kiss deepened and tongues tangled. The heat between them stoked into a flame just as a loud knock sounded at the door, breaking them from their intimate bubble. They both looked at each other, waited a moment, and another insistent knock sounded.

"I'll go see who it is," he said, slipping out of the bed and sliding his jeans back on as he turned to Dee. "Stay right there, I'll be right back."

Jaxon strode towards the door and glanced into the peephole. An attractive older woman stood there looking from side to side, brows pinched together with frustration, before knocking again. Jaxon unlocked the door and opened it slowly, only to be met with the same midnight eyes as Dee.

"Oh!" the woman exclaimed, her hand on her chest as she perused him up and down. "I apologize. I must have the wrong apartment. I'm looking for Devine Jones." she said with a look of confusion on her lovely face.

"Jaxon, who was it?" Dee called from down the hall as she entered the front entrance in nothing but his white T-shirt.

Recoiling with surprise, Dee took in the woman standing in her front entrance and placed her hands on her hips as she exclaimed in question. "Mom! What are you doing here?"

Jaxon, now seeing the uncanny resemblance, watched as Dee's mother turned to her daughter, mirroring her stance like two-gunslingers ready for a shootout. Her mother scrutinized her head to toe glanced back at Jaxon, her eyes unapologetically roaming over his bare torso while he could literally see her put two and two together, as she answered, "I missed you at church this morning, so I decided to come to Primrose to see your new place and perhaps take you out for lunch." She explained, glancing over to Dee again. "But I can see I was interrupting something."

Jaxon wasn't sure how to respond or if he should respond, so his eyes darted towards Dee, hoping she would have the answer. Dee simply laughed and rolled her eyes then walked over to her mother, wrapping her in a big hug as she declared. "As always, Mom, your timing is impeccable."

"Well, I don't think I need permission to drop in on my one and only daughter." She responded with a laugh of her own as she released their embrace and turned to Jaxon. "Are you going to introduce me to your friend?"

Dee walked over to Jaxon, the tightly wound tension in his body just a moment ago easing as she wrapped an arm around his waist. "Mom, this is my boyfriend, Jaxon Isley. Jaxon, this is my mom, Barbara Jones."

Jaxon smiled down at Dee as his gaze drifted to her mother and he put his hand out in greeting. "Hello, Ms. Jones, pleasure to meet you."

"Oh, please call me Barbara, you know, like Streisand." she said, accepting his hand with a wink. "You sure are a handsome one." She said, still holding his hand as she turned to Dee, giving her a chiding look. "And your boyfriend? I was just talking to you last week, and you never mentioned anything about a boyfriend."

"It's new, Mom." Dee replied, rolling her eyes in exasperation.

Her mother turned back to Jaxon and squeezed his hand. "Now that we've met, you need to join us for lunch. I need to get to know you before I can approve of you spending time with my daughter."

"How about I take both of you lovely ladies out for lunch?" Jaxon offered with a smile. "I'm just going to run home; shower and I'll meet you both back here in 30 minutes."

Her mother offered him her sweetest smile and replied, "That would be wonderful, Jaxon."

ONCE JAXON HAD GATHERED his things and left Dee's apartment, her mother turned to her, the look on her face turning from sweet and demure to scolding. Dee knew it was coming. As soon as she saw her mother in her front entrance and a half naked Jaxon beside her, she knew exactly what her mother was going to say.

"When were you going to tell me that you were seeing someone?" she asked, hand on her hip.

"Why do I need to tell you everything I do?" she countered. "I'm a grown ass woman if you haven't realized it."

"I know, sweetheart, but you need to be more cautious. What do you know about this guy?" she asked. "How long have you known him?"

"We met a few weeks ago and Jaxon is 37, is an ex-minor league baseball player and owns his own construction company. He owns this building, in fact, and he's smart, funny, incredibly sweet, and I really like him."

"Well, I can see that!" she said, gesturing to her in nothing but his shirt. "You better be careful, my girl, and not get blinded by lust. Men tend to tell a girl what she wants to hear when she has stars in her eyes."

Dee shook her head, not believing her mother just went there. She had spent her entire life hearing about how her mother was scorned by her father, but that didn't mean she needed to paint all men with the same brush. Over the years, every time Dee told her mother she was dating someone, or even had a date, she would give her a speech on how she should be careful trusting them. She was so tired of her mother trying to project her past experiences onto her, and she wasn't about to let her downplay how she was feeling about this new and exciting relationship with Jaxon.

"Jaxon is a good man and is not like that, mom. And just because my dad hurt you, doesn't mean all men are like him." She replied, knowing she was taking this to a point of no return. "Maybe you felt like my father took advantage of your affections, but Jaxon is not taking advantage of mine. You've raised me to be far too strong to let that happen, so trust me when I say I won't let what happened to you happen to me."

Her mother gave her a look of consternation as she exhaled in dramatic fashion, and raised her chin, her eyes locked on Dee's as she replied, "He'll have to prove himself to me."

"I wouldn't expect anything less." Dee responded with a shake of her head and an exasperated laugh. She reached for her mother's hand and gave it an affectionate squeeze as she requested, "Give Jaxon a chance, and I know for a fact that you will like him as much as I do."

DEE EMERGED FROM HER BEDROOM, showered, and dressed, ready for lunch with her mother and her impossibly handsome new boyfriend. Hearing laughter in her kitchen, she stopped just outside her bedroom, taking in her mother's singsong laugh and Jaxon's deep rich one filling the open space of her apartment. Curious, she hung back in the hallway for a moment to listen to their conversation.

"Dee was just so cute in that commercial. It only took her three takes to get her lines right, and the director said he had never worked with such a naturally talented kid," her mother bragged. "My daughter has always been a star. She lights up every camera and stage she graces."

"I think I remember that commercial," Jaxon replied. "And I have to agree. She has a way of lighting up every room."

Dee beamed as she walked into the kitchen, a playful smirk on her face. "I mean, I know how awesome I am, but a girl can never get enough compliments."

"Speaking of light, you look gorgeous." Jaxon complimented, taking in her casual black jeans, green cashmere sweater and bright yellow ballet flats. She had wrapped her braids up in a colorful scarf which her mother had given her for her recent birthday.

"Why thank you J." she said, going on her tiptoes to give him a chaste kiss before wrapping her arms around his waist.

Her mother's eyes darted from her to him a few times as a smile slowly bloomed on her face. A face telling Dee all she needed to know. Her mother undoubtedly approved of Jaxon.

CHAPTER 6

After such a whirlwind weekend, Jaxon wasn't sure how to bring his focus back to his workday. All morning, he found himself distracted by thoughts of Dee and their incredible two days together. Last night he spent the night again, both not wanting the weekend to end. This morning, he drove her to work, giving her a lingering kiss before she climbed out of his truck and flashed him her heart stopping dimpled smile. Everything about being with Dee felt natural and domestic, like they had been together for years.

The door opened and his longtime friend, Hayden Hastings, strode in, greeting Davis, then peeking into Jaxon's office.

"Hey J, are you down for lunch at the Eazy? Davis and I are about to walk over there."

"Yeah, sure," he replied, closing his laptop and getting up from his desk. Grabbing his jacket, he met Hayden and Davis in the front entrance and, as they exited, he pulled out his keys to lock the door to the office.

The men made their way down the sidewalk to the Eazy Café, which was everyone's go-to stop for greasy diner food. When inside they spotted a free booth at the back and claimed it as the lunch rush descended on this town hot spot. Placing their orders, they settled back in the booth and Hayden's curious gaze rested on Jaxon as he commented, "Someone came into the store today, saying they spotted you yesterday with a certain lovely new drama teacher."

Here we go. He knew Primrose and how the infamous gossip mill worked around here, so he was sure it was only a matter of time before word spread about his relationship with Dee.

"Yeah, I was having lunch with Dee and her mother," he said matter of fact as he took a sip of his coke.

Davis laughed and clapped him on the shoulder. "First date to meeting the mother, all in one weekend? Well done, my friend."

Hayden's eyes flitted from Jaxon to Davis and back to Jaxon, with an incredulous look on his face. "Wait, what? So, is the rumor true? You and Dee Jones are a thing? How is this the first I've heard of this?"

"It's new." Jaxon shared with a shrug, his lips curling into a smile. "Dee and I are dating and she's actually my girlfriend."

Davis let out a bountiful laugh as he commented. "You're a fast mover."

Hayden sat back and let out a low whistle, as he shook his head, and a smile curved his lips. "You and Dee Jones. I never would've thought. Isn't she a lot younger than you?"

"10 years." Jaxon replied.

"Wow, okay that's not bad," Hayden mused as he repeated, "You and Dee Jones. I've only met her once at Savanah and Rami's wedding and she's an absolute riot. Huge personality and super fun to be around. Very beautiful too." he nodded in approval. "Good on you J."

"I've gotten to know her through Savanah, and I personally think she'll be good for you. Shake up your life a little bit. Honestly man, your life needs a little shake up," Davis added.

Hayden nodded in agreement.

Jaxon took in Davis's words. *Does my life need a shake up?* He'd been alone for so long; he really didn't realize what he was missing until this weekend. It had been so easy after Leah betrayed his trust to just shut himself off from his emotions and all romantic relationships. Far too easy to tell himself he didn't need a woman in his life and the only person he could trust was himself. Dee made him want to try it all again, to open himself up to the possibility of more.

"I really like her," he confessed. "I feel like I can breathe again when I'm with her, and she makes me think about the future again. About all the possibilities."

"Whoa! Who are you and what have you done with Jaxon?" Hayden laughed, leaning back against the vinyl bench of their booth.

Jaxon leaned onto the table and shook his head. "I think I'm starting to fall for her."

"Damn." Davis commented. "That must've been some date."

"It was," he added, looking off wistfully. "She just has this light about her that completely draws me in," he shared, as he ran his hand through his hair and down his stubbled chin, as he let out a laugh. "Am I crazy to feel this strong for her so soon?"

"When you know you know," Hayden answered. "I knew Whitney was who I wanted to be with the first time I met her. Literally we locked eyes, and I knew."

"It didn't take me long either." Davis added. "Two weeks in a house with Marnie and I wanted to play house for the rest of our lives."

"Are you thinking about lifetime stuff here?" Hayden asked curiously.

"Honestly, I'm not sure I want to get married again." Jaxon confessed. "Leah really messed up my views on marriage and after her, I sort of swore I never would again."

"Never say never," Davis replied with a shrug.

Would I ever consider getting married again? He asked himself. It's not like he didn't believe in the sanctity of marriage. He had the best possible example with his parents. Yet the thought of heading down that path again honestly gave him heart palpitations. You don't need a formal wedding and a marriage to start a life with someone else. Lots of people in committed relationships just lived together, opting not to make it official. He needed to put that thought to the back of his mind. Thinking about marriage felt like a trigger for him, and he had no idea where Dee stood on things. Plus, it was far too early to consider forever.

* * *

GARRETT WALKED into the drama room around lunchtime with his lunch bag in his hands. "Hey, Dee! How are the musical preparations going?" he asked, grabbing a chair and setting it across from her desk.

"Ah-mazing!" Dee exclaimed, offering her friend and fellow teacher an excited smile. "This afternoon, we start with song practice, and I have a class with just the main cast members to go through scenes. Oh, and Jaxon is coming on Friday to start building the sets."

"That all sounds fantastic." He said, taking a seat and pulling a sandwich out of his lunch bag. "Speaking of Jaxon, did my eyes deceive me or was that an Isley Construction truck dropping you off at work this morning?"

Dee let out a raspy laugh. *You were expecting someone to notice.* She was well aware that the tongues in town would be wagging when they found out that she and Jaxon were an item. She reached into her desk and pulled out an apple and a container with salad in it. "Yes, that was Jaxon's truck." She replied, a mirthful smile on her lips. "Jaxon Isley and I are seeing each other."

Garrett's smile grew wide, and he nodded his head in approval at this new tidbit of information. "Nice guy. I met him last summer at Hayden and Whitney Hastings housewarming. He did a great job on their renovations. He's very quiet, though. Kind of the opposite of you," he teased, kicking her foot playfully under the desk.

Dee laughed and kicked him back. "You know what they say. Opposites attract." She replied, as she bit her lip and met Garrett's gaze. "I'm pretty sure I am falling for him already."

Garrett's eyes widened as he surveyed her, then his expression turned to one of curiosity. He leaned forward, resting his elbows on the desk as he asked, "Have you ever felt like this before, for someone?

"No, but it's all happening so quickly with J. I literally can't stop thinking about him, and I want to be around him all the time. He exudes this air of true, honest goodness and when I'm around him he makes me feel special," she replied with a swoony sigh. "And the way he looks at me…" Dee paused dramatically as she pinned Garrett with her love drunk stare. "…no one has ever looked at me like that."

"And so, it begins." Garrett said with a knowing smile. "That's the way all great love stories start."

Dee smiled at his comment. *Is this the beginning of our love story? Is Jaxon the one and only person meant for me?* This whole relationship was so new, but she couldn't help but feel hopeful. Like somehow fate had aligned their paths. Whatever happened between her and Jaxon, she couldn't wait to find out how their story would unfold.

PRIMROSE HIGH WAS BUZZING with excitement as musical practice began. Today was all about choreography and choral practice and Dee had assembled her dream team to help her, having recruited her long-time friends, Oliver Boyce, to do the choreography and Emersyn Bridger to do the vocal training. She also brought in Steve Furgallo, the keyboardist for Prairie Sound, who until recently she had no idea was a complete piano savant. With this knowledge and knowing he and his band were on a hiatus from touring and in the middle of recording their second album, she cashed in a favor and talked him into taking over as the accompanist. As she surveyed the scene in the gym, watching her dream team do their thing, she couldn't help but think, *we are going to blow Primrose's mind with this production!*

"Great job, you guys! Seriously, well done memorizing those lines. Remember Danny, to enunciate those words. I know it's a tongue twister, but we want everyone, even those at the back of the room, to hear each word." She said, looking at her 12th grade Gene Kelly. Then, turning to an eager 11th grader, she continued her constructive critique, "And you, Carter, don't forget you are Cosmo Brown, Don Lockwood's best pal. We need to feel that comradery." The boys looked at each other and one put out his fist to bump. "Okay, now go across the gym to see Oliver and he's going to take you through the dance steps for that number." The boys ran off, chattering with each other as they went to where Oliver was waiting for them.

"Looks like you're taking over my space already." Anders' smug voice sounded behind her.

Dee internally groaned as she glanced his way and squinted at him with annoyance. Turning to face him, she put her hands on her hips, taking on a warrior stance and giving him a look of challenge as she replied, "Yes, it looks like it. But don't worry Anders, we'll be out of your hair at 4 p.m. today." She informed, feigning a smile.

Anders stepped towards her, uncomfortably close and in her space, his hands casually in his pockets. With an arrogant smirk on his face, he said, "I saw Jaxon Isley drop you off this morning."

Dee narrowed her eyes further. *Where's he going with this? You need to look unphased and stand your ground.* "Yes, that's what thoughtful boyfriends do." She replied. *Take that gym boy.*

Anders laughed a huge guffaw of a laugh as he continued in a mocking tone, "Boyfriend? Really Dee? You turn me down and go for a guy like that?" He looked away for a moment with his question and she could literally see him seethe. Turning back to her, his eyes burning with anger, he added, "Now I guess I know your type."

She glared at him, anger rising in her chest at his condescending tone as she replied, "Yeah, what type is that, Anders?"

"Old, washed-up athletes." He replied with a cocky grin on his smug face.

Dee was livid, but she wasn't going to give him the satisfaction of getting the last word. Approaching him and getting right into his face, she gritted her teeth, her voice low and controlled as she replied, "Just because I found myself, a real man, instead of going out with a jerk like you, doesn't mean you have the right to put down someone I care about."

Stepping away from him, she turned just as the gym door opened, and Jaxon and Hayden walked into the gym carrying sheets of plywood meant for building the sets. Dee glanced over her shoulder and gave Anders one more challenging glare before she turned her attention to Jaxon and Hayden and softened into a greeting smile. She caught Anders in her peripheral as he sauntered away, his arrogant grin still on his face. *That's right, walk away, you jerk.*

"Just set those against the wall over there." She directed, pointing towards the far wall. The men did as she asked and strode back over to her. Jaxon put his arm around Dee, and she curled into his side, needing his hug after her heated encounter with the egotistical gym teacher. The delicious warmth of Jaxon's body and smell of his cologne instantly soothing her frustration. Glancing up at him with affection, she drawled, "Hey there, Cowboy."

"Hi." he replied with a smile as he leaned down and planted a kiss on her hair, making her audibly sigh in response.

Hayden looked from Jaxon to Dee with a huge grin on his face. "Hey, there Dee! Not sure if you remember me, I'm Hayden Hastings."

"Of course, I remember you!" she laughed, pulling him in for a friendly hug. "You had all the moves on the dance floor at Rami and Savanah's wedding."

Hayden let out a laugh and replied, "That was a fun night."

"Hayden and I went to school together, and he's one of my closest friends." Jaxon shared as he grinned at his longtime friend.

"Ah, okay, it's so funny how these small towns work, everyone knowing everyone. I'm sure you two have some interesting stories about growing up here." She said with a wink. "Two rambunctious boys getting into trouble."

Hayden laughed, "We sure do! Speaking of knowing everyone in a small town, I don't think I know that guy you were talking to," he mentioned as he gestured over to Anders.

Dee glanced Anders' way, seeing he was still lingering around, obviously keeping an eye on her and Jaxon. She turned back and rolled her eyes with a frown. "That's the gym teacher, Anders Barick. He's not from here and I'm honestly not sure where he's from, but he's been making things difficult for me."

"How so?" Jaxon asked, his brows furrowing as his eyes flitted towards Anders.

"Just not wanting to give me space for practice, telling me I'm in his territory and that I owe him. All together, just being a jerk. He's been asking me out every week since I took this job and I started out turning him down gently until I had enough. The week before we started dating, I basically told him to back off." She shared, looking up at Jaxon and glancing at Hayden, then leaning in, whispering. "He thinks he's God's gift to womankind and honestly…" she leaned in, lowering her voice further. "…he's an arrogant douchebag."

Hayden burst out laughing, but Jaxon looked down at Dee with a look of concern on his face.

She glanced up at him and gave him a reassuring smile as she said, "Don't worry. I can hold my own with him, and I know who to go to if he gets out of hand."

CHAPTER 7

Jaxon carried in the last of the plywood he needed to start building the sets in the gym. It was 4 p.m. on Friday and most of the school had cleared out except for a few teachers visiting after their classes and the janitor. The gym was quiet and although all he wanted was to spend his evening with Dee; he had made her a promise that he would get a head start on the sets she needed built. Setting up a portable worktable, he rolled out the plans he drew up for the sets and he started framing out the walls of the four rooms that would become the backdrop for the main scenes of the play. Having never seen *Singin' in the Rain* in its entirety, he did his homework, first asking Dee what she envisioned and then watching the film to get an idea as to the aesthetic. He had to admit after watching the movie; he got excited thinking about their little school recreating it on their small-town stage. Dee had her work cut out for her, but he had no doubt if anyone could make it happen, it would be his girl.

"I hope you're going to clean up this mess when you're done?" A man's voice sounded behind him, disrupting his thoughts.

Jaxon looked up from what he was doing to see the gym teacher, Anders, leaning against the wall, legs crossed, and arms folded over his wide chest. He had a smug look on his face, and Jaxon could feel the ego ooze from him. Standing up straight, Jaxon replied, "Of course."

"Good, because this crap is taking up too much of my space," he said, unfolding his arms and striding over to where Jaxon was working. "Seriously, who needs a musical, anyways? Such a waste of time and money."

Jaxon didn't look up and let his comment slide off his back. Even though he knew for certain if Dee was here, she would have given him a piece of her mind. He continued to measure out the piece and reached for his circular saw, quickly cutting the piece to the size he needed.

"What's that pretty girlfriend of yours doing tonight?" Anders continued, his voice dripping with insolence. He laughed and added, "Or should I ask, who's she doing tonight?" He came closer to Jaxon, his voice at his back. "You know she flirts with everyone, right? I wouldn't be surprised if you were one of many."

Jaxon could feel the steam rise between his ears with his words, as he was very aware how easy and satisfying it would be to turn around and slug the guy in the jaw or perhaps give him a black eye. However, he could tell this guy was simply trying to get a rise out of him and he wasn't about to give him the satisfaction. Anders was obviously privy to his story and was taking a low blow to get a reaction. *Asshole.*

Besides, Jaxon knew Dee was over at her friend Savanah's house tonight and he was picking her up after he was done the framing. *So nice try buddy.* Whatever dating experience she had prior to their relationship was none of his business, as he too had his fair share of experience and considered it hypocritical for him to judge anyone on their past.

"I don't know, Jaxon. You better watch her closely, or she's bound to move on to someone else," he warned, making one last attempt at shaking Jaxon's insecurities. Jaxon remained stoic, steading his thoughts, not giving Anders any satisfaction of a response.

Not getting the reaction he wanted, Anders randomly threw out as he went. "I guess Dee prefers washed up losers to real men."

Jaxon tamped down the insult, proud of himself for keeping his cool and let out a long exhale once Anders was gone. *If Anders is like this with me, a stranger to him, how is he with Dee?* Jaxon had no doubt, his girlfriend was tough, and he would never question that she could hold her own with a jerk like Anders, but it pained him to think about her having to deal with such conflict on a daily basis. *I guess I'm going to have to keep my eye on Anders Barick.*

Friday night at Casa Perez did not disappoint. With Rami having a rare Friday night off, he offered to cook them a Mexican feast with margaritas rather than their usual wine and cheese plate. With the smell of spicy chilis, tomatillos, slow cooked chicken and citrus in the air, Dee knew she was in for a much-needed night of comfort food and fun with her bestie and her beau. Dee needed to unwind and unpack the course of the past week with her best friend, and since Rami had become close to her as well, she had no problem having him join in on their conversation.

"Okay, tell me about this, Jaxon. I've seen him around town, but honestly, I've never met him." Rami urged, hovering over a large pot of heavenly smelling chili verde.

"What do you all want to know?" Dee asked with a laugh as she took a sip of her margarita, letting the tart lime and tequila swirl in her mouth.

"Everything!" Rami exclaimed. "Spill the tea girl!"

Savanah and Dee laughed, loving Rami's rather shameful attempt at being one of the girls tonight.

"Okay, okay, where to start?" Dee asked, tapping her chin. "Well, as you know he owns Isley Construction and the building I live in. He literally lives right next door to me."

"That's convenient." Rami laughed, waggling his eyebrows.

Dee gave him a wink in agreement as she continued, "He's tall, dark, and ruggedly handsome. A total country boy which is totally the opposite of me, as you know, but weirdly I find it completely hot. He's calm, laidback, so incredibly sweet, and he makes me feel like a queen." She answered.

"Which you are of course!" Savanah exclaimed with a giggle as she curtsied, then stumbled a little, causing her to splash some of her margarita onto the countertop.

"Whoa, there lightweight." Rami said, catching her and pulling her into his arms. "As cute as you are when you've been drinking, I may have to take this away from you," he said slowly, sliding her glass away from her reach and making Dee laugh as he pulled Savanah in for a chaste kiss.

Dee sighed as she watched her dear friends. Rami and Savanah were couple goals for sure. She had seen their journey to where they were now, having been childhood friends, to teenage crushes, to reuniting, to falling in love, then tragically breaking up, and finally finding their way back to each other and becoming each other's happily ever. If you looked up soul mates in the dictionary, she was sure their pictures would be there.

The doorbell rang and Dee brightened as she hopped off her stool excitedly, knowing exactly who was at the door. Making her way into their front entrance, she opened the door to see her sexy boyfriend, looking deliciously rugged in a plaid shirt, torn jeans, and a ball cap. She grinned up at him, his ocean blue eyes twinkling in the porch lights. "Hey there, Cowboy." she purred coquettishly as she launched herself into his arms, hooked her arms around his neck and wrapped her legs around his waist.

"Now that's a hello," he said, planting a long languid kiss on her lips as he squeezed her behind. Pulling back, he licked his lips, as a grin curled up his mouth and he asked,

"Margaritas?"

She nodded. "Do I taste good?" she asked flirtatiously as she leaned in and kissed him again, her tongue slipping into his mouth sliding against his.

He breathlessly pulled his head back again and answered her question. "Delicious."

"Speaking of delicious. Rami is cooking tonight." She said, unwrapping herself from him as he set her down on her feet and she grabbed his hand. "Come meet my friends." Pulling him into the kitchen, Rami and Savanah smiled in greeting. "Jaxon, these are two of my closest friends, Ramiro and Savanah Perez."

"Nice to meet you." Rami said, offering his hand to shake. "Call me Rami."

Savanah offered Jaxon her hand to shake as well. "Welcome to our home."

"Thank you." Jaxon replied as he removed his cap and took a seat next to Dee at the kitchen island. Savanah gave Dee a sly thumbs up with a wink, making her smile. "It smells amazing in here."

Rami beamed, "Thanks, I have a rare Friday night off from performing, so when I do, I like to cook. Tonight, we have chili verde with homemade tortillas on the menu and I made the ladies some margaritas. Would you like a cerveza or if you prefer a margarita, I can mix you one," Rami offered as he stirred the pot and turned off the burner.

"A cerveza sounds great." Jaxon replied as Savanah reached into the refrigerator and handed him a cold beer. He flashed her a smile of thanks as he twisted off the cap.

Rami picked up his beer and clinked his with Jaxon's. "Here's to good food, new friends and seeing Dee stupidly happy."

The men brought their beers to their mouths to take a sip, and Rami gave Dee a quick wink. Her lips curved up and Jaxon put his hand on her thigh as his gaze met hers, his eyes sparkling with adoration and deep affection. *I will never get tired of how he looks at me.*

"Dinner's ready!" Rami exclaimed as he brought the pot of chili over to the table that was set for four. Dee leaned in, feeling the delicious scruff of his stubble on her cheek, her hot breath at his ear. "I missed you today. Can I come over to your place tonight?"

He grinned, his eyes flashing with desire as he replied, "I was hoping you would ask."

JAXON CARRIED Dee into his apartment, and he glanced down at her fast asleep in his arms. It was late and Dee had fallen asleep on the short ride home. With a full belly of delicious food and a few too many margaritas, as soon as he heard her slow steady breaths when he pulled into the parking lot, he knew that his girlfriend was asleep. *My girlfriend.* Saying that still felt strange. He hadn't had a girlfriend in over a decade and the label felt so different now that he was older. The word girlfriend carried so much more meaning. He wasn't dating just to date and have fun. He had a long game to think of. He wasn't getting any younger, and he still believed in commitment.

Whether that commitment looked like marriage, he didn't know. But what he did know right now, is he could see Dee being part of his future.

Tonight, she had shared yet another part of herself with him. She introduced him to two of her closest friends. Two people she respected and had a history with, and they couldn't have been more welcoming to him. By the end of their evening of conversation and laughter, he was certain he had gained two new friends himself and the fact that their lives were starting to intertwine filled him with a warmth and security he didn't realize he needed.

Dee stirred in his arms and buried her head in his chest as he carried her into his bedroom. Setting her on the bed, she opened her eyes briefly and smiled up at him, her adorable dimples making an appearance.

"Can I get you undressed for bed?" he asked. "I want you to be comfortable."

She nodded as he made short work of undressing her and grabbing a t-shirt from his dresser. Slipping it on her, he pulled back the covers for her to slide in. Crouching down, he brushed her braids away from her face and smiled as he took in her beauty. Every time he looked at Dee, his heart opened and filled with this insatiable need to take care of her. It wasn't that she needed anyone to take care of her, as she was more than capable of taking care of herself. But he couldn't help but want to keep her close and protect her. Leaning in, he kissed her cheek softly, and she sighed, snuggling deeper into the pillow as he rose to his feet. Heading into his ensuite, he got ready for bed and grabbed the wastebasket, a glass of water and a few Tylenols, setting them on her nightstand next to her sleeping form. *She's going to feel that tequila in the morning.*

Sliding in behind her, he curled around the curve of her body, his face in her hair and hand on the swell of her hip. He inhaled deeply; her intoxicating scent comforting him. She was so warm and soft to his touch, and he lay there in the dark, relishing the feeling of her against him. Thinking back, he couldn't remember a time when he felt so content. Even when he was married. He loved Leah but, in the years they were together, she had made it very clear that she only wanted his affection on her terms. He spent so many nights either on the opposite side of the bed or on the couch. She never liked him holding or cuddling her. Then there were the countless nights where she said she was staying with friends after a girl's night out. He should have known back then that something was up, as the red flags were all there. Having experienced the betrayal of cheating, he spent far too many years carrying around a self-deprecating attitude, thinking he was never going to be enough for someone else and thinking there was something innately wrong with him. Then, when he least expected it, this beautiful woman splashed into his life, quite literally coming out of nowhere and making him feel like more than enough. Making him feel wanted, needed, and wholly desired. Feelings he didn't even realize he was missing. Dee wriggled into the groove of his body, and he smiled as he inhaled her sweetness again, closed his eyes and drifted off into a contented sleep.

* * *

THERE ARE nice ways to wake up and then there are delightfully naughty ways to wake up. Like this morning as she writhed herself awake, the sweet burn of her desire building in her core, her eyes opening to Jaxon's shaggy head between her legs, his tongue doing wickedly magical things to her. She reached for him, her fingers feathering through his soft hair as she moaned in approval. "You are so amazing at this," she rasped, rocking into his mouth. Taking her nub of pleasure between his lips and slipping two fingers inside her finding the coveted spot, she cried out loudly as she gave into the white-hot pleasure of her release. As she came down from her orgasm, he climbed over her, his chin glistening with her arousal, looking justifiably proud of himself. She pulled him in for a hot, erotic kiss, tasting herself on his lips. Sliding his hard length through her aching folds, he smiled, a sexy, lust drunk smile. "Good morning, Beautiful."

"Good morning." She rasped, smoothing the hair that flopped into his eyes.

"Are you feeling okay this morning?", he asked, his brows drawn together in question. "You had a lot to drink and fell asleep on the way home. I carried you to bed."

"I feel amazing. I've just discovered the best cure for hangovers." She said with a playful twinkle in her eyes.

"What's that?"

"Orgasms." she replied with a sexy smile curving her lips.

He lowered his head to kiss her as he slid into her body with a long, deep thrust. She moaned against his lips as he continued to devour her mouth, capturing her gasps and cries as he handed her yet another magnificent O. *Best way to wake up ever.*

"The best hangover cure, in my opinion..." Jaxon started, as he pulled out a turner from the drawer. "...are grilled cheese sandwiches."

"I thought we established that great sex was the remedy." Dee laughed, giving him a playful wink. "Which, by the way, you administered perfectly."

"Your theory has definite merit, although I think we need to do a lot more beta testing on the orgasm theory," he replied with a smirk. "For now, I present to you the PG cure all, my infamous grilled cheese." He flipped a sandwich up and caught it on a plate in midair, making Dee clap and laugh with delight before he presented it to her. "Ladies first."

Dee picked up the delicious-looking sandwich, the steam wafting from it as she took a bite, the molten cheese burning her lip. She put down the sandwich and touched her lip, then laughed. "Too hot," she mumbled with the bite in her mouth.

Jaxon turned off the burner of the stove and came around the island, turning her to face him. "Where does it hurt?" he whispered.

Dee glanced up at him through her long lashes and darted her tongue out to touch the sensitive spot where the cheese burned her.

He smiled and bent down to gently kiss the spot as he caged her against the island. His hot hard body, making her pulse quicken and heart flutter wildly. "Better?" he asked, so close his breath mingled with hers.

She jutted out her lip in a feigning pout as she replied, "Still hurts."

He laughed and waggled his eyebrows at her. "I got the remedy," he replied as he lifted her over his shoulder caveman style and carried her to the bedroom, Dee squealing with delight.

CHAPTER 8

*D*ee was in a love bubble. A place where the only blissful love, lust and mind-blowing sex could exist. Two weekends spent together with Jaxon, and she never wanted to emerge. The passion between them was addictive, and all she wanted was to stay wrapped up in his strong arms and curled around his hot body. Even when she put aside their palpable sexual chemistry, what they were sharing had so much more depth than the physical. Jaxon was so open with her, not hiding his past and sharing pieces of him as they got to know each other better. Although he was quiet and very much the yin to her yang, she loved his calming, introspective nature. He had a sharp wit and was so damn funny she found her cheeks hurt from all the laughter. Every moment she spent with him, her feelings grew and planted roots, both scaring and exciting her in equal measure.

As the week progressed, the musical practice continued, with Dee working during school hours and after with students to help them perfect their parts. Steve and

Emersyn gave of their time when they could to help the choir as well as her Don Lockwood, Cosmo Brown and Kathy Selden characters practice their songs. And so far, everything sounded amazing. Oliver had her cast tackling choreography that even some of the most talented dancers found challenging, yet her students were enthusiastic and worked hard to memorize each step. She looked at the energetic buzz and commotion around her and smiled with pride. The vision she had for this production was starting to take shape.

Her only obstacle was the persistent harassment getting thrown at her by Anders. He kept hovering over their practices, his arms crossed over his chest, an intimidating, arrogant look on his face. He had made rude inappropriate comments to her team and little uncalled for jabs. They had brought these comments to Dee, and she immediately took them to the principal, who had a discussion with Anders. Unfortunately, it became obvious that he had told them what they wanted to hear as nothing was done to stop him from continuing his relentless pestering. Frustrated and annoyed, she decided to focus on something she could control and escaped into the costume closet to take inventory of what they needed for the production.

"Dee, are you in here?" Jaxon's voice sounded as she heard the door open.

"I am! Back here!" she exclaimed. Jaxon appeared around a rack of clothing, looking rugged and sexy as always. "Hey hot stuff." Dee greeted, putting her arms around his waist, and looking up at him. "Are you here to work on the sets?"

"I am, and I was wondering if you wanted to help me. I brought pizza and thought it might be fun," he said with a twinkle in his eye.

"You mean I get to play with your tools?" she asked with a laugh as she threw out a flirty innuendo.

"I believe you already know how to play with my tool," he said, backing her into the far wall and caging her in. He looked around, glancing in the corners. "No security cameras here?"

"Not in here." She replied, biting her bottom lip, as she reached for the waistband of his jeans and flicked open the top button. Sliding her hand inside, she gripped his hard steel, making a low growl rumble from his throat.

His eyes turning dark with desire as she stroked him, his hips rocking into her hands as he took control and lifted her, her legs hooked around him and her back pressed against the cinderblock wall. Her pencil skirt bunched up around her thighs, as he kissed her hard and ground her core with his ridge, making her moan. "I need you, Jaxon."

Pushing down his jeans and boxers, his length of him now free, he pumped between their bodies before shifting her panties to the side, positioning himself, and sinking home. They both gasped in pleasure as he took control, pumping deep into her body. Their moans, along with the sound of their bodies connecting, echoed within the confined space and she buried her face in his neck, trying to control her involuntary noises as he took her hard, fast, and dirty against the wall.

"Jaxon, oh god," she whimpered, her body tightening,

pulsing in waves of pleasure as they both found their release.

Breathless and disheveled, Jaxon rested his forehead against hers, their chests heaving as they tried to steady themselves. They stood for a moment, still connected, Dee's back pressed up to the wall as she was held up by Jaxon, their eyes locked on each other. Something flashed in Jaxon's eyes, and Dee immediately saw it. *Is that concern?*

"What's wrong?" Dee rasped, gripping his face, trying to search his gaze.

"We didn't use protection," he replied. "Oh, Dee, fuck, I know better," he said, breaking their connection and lowering her to her feet.

She straightened out her skirt and met his worried gaze, giving him a reassuring look as she touched his arm. "I should be okay. J. Chances are slim to none that I can get pregnant anyways, and I'm clean."

"I'm clean too," he replied quickly, yet still lingering in a state of panic as he ran his hand through his messy hair.

"Seriously, J, I'm not upset," she repeated, wrapping her arms around him. "I don't even know if I can get pregnant." He gave her a quizzical look, and she elaborated. "I have something called Polycystic Ovary Syndrome. It is an endocrine disorder, where my brain can't give my body the message to ovulate each month so it can make getting pregnant very difficult." She answered. "I was told I only have a 5% chance of getting pregnant without some kind of fertility intervention."

He stared at her a beat, his brows knitting together and his eyes softening with compassion. "I'm sorry, Dee."

he said, touching her face and raising her chin to him. He looked at her and she could see he was trying to find the right words to respond to this new tidbit of information. He asked carefully, "Do you have options if you ever want to have kids?"

"I do. I can go on medication that could correct the problem as well as fertility drugs. Then if that doesn't work, there are more invasive fertility treatments like IVF. Either way, it would be a difficult process to get pregnant. I guess if I was in a relationship where we both wanted a family, it would be a process worth going through," she said, shrugging, then glancing away, feeling buried emotions start to rise. She cleared her throat to steady herself and she looked up to meet his sensitive gaze, her throat tightening painfully.

Having been diagnosed with PCOS in her early twenties, finding out her chances were a meager 5% filled her with a deep sadness she wasn't expecting. A newfound desire to have something she never knew she wanted until she was told she may not have it at all. Years later, she had become resolute about motherhood, accepting that it may not be in the cards for her. Now, though, standing in front of a man she was starting to fall in love with and talking about it, that repressed sadness she felt on the day of diagnosis threatened to resurface. *Does he even want kids? Is fatherhood part of his trajectory? I need to ask.*

"Do you want to have kids someday?" she asked, meeting his gaze.

"Yes, God willing," he replied, with no hesitation. "If it's with someone I love and care deeply for. Although if

I'm being honest, I'm not sure I want to get married again."

She nodded, feeling her stomach sink a little at his candid admission. She understood where his apprehension came from, knowing what she now knew of his past. *But has he given up on lifetime commitment all together?*

As if reading her mind and seeing the barrage of questions running through her head, he added, "Even if I'm unsure of marriage, I do want the commitment of being with one person for the rest of my life."

Am I okay with that? Can I be with someone knowing that marriage wasn't on the table? One look in his blue gaze and Dee had her answer. "I want that too."

"Seems we're on the same page then." He confirmed, a slow smile curling his lips. She nodded as he cupped her face and leaned down, tenderly brushing his lips to hers. Something about his kiss felt like a promise to her. A promise that even if he didn't know what the future looked like just yet, he wanted his future to be with her.

AS THE WEEKS WENT ON, they grew closer, spending every night in each other's arms. The comfort and familiarity of having her in his space turned into something he craved. She was addictive to be around and every time they were apart, even for a short time; he needed a hit. Every part of her brightened his day, and he could feel the familiar feelings of love bloom in his chest. *Does she feel the same?* Every time he questioned, or doubt surfaced, all he had to do was look into her eyes to get his answers. There was love there, he was certain of it.

His phone rang, and he smiled, recognizing the number immediately. Accepting the call, he answered, "Hey Mom!"

"Jax, my dear boy, how are you?" his mother asked with so much joy in her expression, he couldn't help but smile. He adored his mom. She was so warm and nurturing and had the patience of a saint when it came to him and his brothers. Raising five boys was enough to test the will of most, and she made it look effortless with her firm hand and kind heart.

"I'm great, Mom!" he answered, knowing there was a reason for this out of the blue call and he was sure he knew exactly what that reason was.

"I've been waiting and waiting for you to come to me first, but since you still haven't called me, I'm just going to come right out and ask," she informed, chiding in her tone. *Here we go. A parental dressing down and a guilt trip. Well done, mom.* "All the ladies at my quilting group have been asking me if I've met your girlfriend yet, and I don't know what to tell them, Jaxon. You haven't even told me about her yet!" she scolded in a way only a loving mother could.

His front door opened, and Dee strode in, causing him to pause at the sight of her. Every time he laid eyes on his girlfriend, his heart started beating rapidly against his chest and the words, *she's all mine,* floated through his consciousness. She walked over to him, rested her hands on his stomach and went on her tiptoes to plant a chaste kiss on his lips. "Hi" she whispered with that sweet little rasp he loved so much.

"Jaxon, are you there? You went quiet for a moment there." His mother asked, frustration edging her voice.

"Sorry, Mom, yes, I'm still here and no, I wasn't trying to hide her from you and Dad." he replied, mouthing to Dee that he was talking to his mom. "We've just been super busy."

"You work far too much, Jaxon. No excuses! You're coming over for Dinner Saturday night. Cade is returning home on Friday from Ottawa and all your brothers can come for dinner, so I insist you and your new beau come, too."

"Sure Mom. Dee and I will be there on Saturday night," he said as Dee smiled and gave him a thumbs up.

"Good!" she exclaimed. "See you Saturday, sweetheart."

"See you then, Mom." he replied as he hung up.

Setting his phone down, he looked across the island at Dee and reached out for her hand, threading his fingers through hers. "Are you ready, Ms. Jones, to be subjected to a night with the Isleys?"

She cocked an eyebrow at him and flashed him her gorgeous, dimpled smile. "I can't wait."

JAXON AND DEE drove up to a country property just a mile east of Primrose. A huge white country home with an open front porch came into view as they drove down the long driveway and parked next to the house. The yard was sprawling, with large oak trees speckled throughout the expansive yard and evergreens framing the property.

"This is where you grew up?" Dee asked, her eyes wide as she unbuckled her seatbelt. "It's like a storybook house," she said as she took in the large two-story home, with a winding front porch and brick chimney stack.

"It's a pretty magical place." He replied, climbing out of the truck and meeting her at the front of his vehicle. Lacing his hand through hers, he pointed to a large oak tree whose branches spread out over the side of the yard. "My brothers and I used to climb that tree and it drove my mother crazy with worry. It's any wonder we're all still alive as we were all a bunch of daredevils." he said with a chuckle "And you see that open corner over there..." he turned to the opposite side of the yard that was all open space and pointed to the corner. "...my dad made us a baseball diamond to practice over there." He smiled, looking wistful as he added, "I bet the bases are still there."

Dee glanced up at him, the happiness and nostalgia for his childhood home radiating through his smile, and she could almost hear the sweet laughter of children playing in the yard. "I can see it's a special place." She commented, so grateful that he brought her here. "I love it."

Jaxon cupped her cheek with affection and leaned down, kissing her chastely as he whispered. "I'm so glad you're here." Squeezing her hand, they made their way down the walkway and as they approached the house, the front door flew open. Four tall, handsome dark-haired men bounded out of the house, charging at Jaxon and making Dee reflexively let go of his hand to step out of the way. One floppy haired man jumped on his back, one with wavy haired man started punching his arm, one wearing a beanie had him in a headlock and was mussing up his hair and the fourth with big blue eyes was doubled over laughing as the others attempted to tackle him to the ground. Dee stood back, both surprised and completely amused as she took in the scene of five grown men acting like wild and unruly children.

"Boys, stop acting like a bunch of buffoons! We have a guest tonight," a beautiful slim white-haired woman with straight shoulder length hair shouted from her perch on the front porch. She was flagged by a very handsome older man with white hair, a trim white beard, and bright blue eyes. The woman turned her gaze to Dee and her smile grew wide as she descended the stairs and strode right over to her. "You must be Devine." she said, pulling her in for a hug. "We're huggers around here, so you better get used to it," she said before releasing her and holding her out at arm's length. "We're so happy to have you here with us tonight. My infuriating son here..." she began, turning to Jaxon and giving him a chiding look. "... has been keeping you all to himself. So, I apologize that it's taken us so long to finally meet."

Dee smiled at Jaxon, who was now hugging each of his brothers, and he winked back at her. "No apology necessary, and thank you for inviting me, Mrs. Isley."

"Please call me Rose." she said, letting go of her and gesturing to the man next to her. "And this is my husband, Robert."

The man next to her was tall and lean, with broad shoulders like all his sons. It was immediately clear to Dee that the apples did not fall far from the tree, as he, too, was very handsome. "Nice to meet you, Dee." he said in a low, rich voice as he pulled her in for another hug, making her feel all warm and fuzzy inside.

Stepping back from his embrace, she turned to Jaxon and the four men standing next to him, put her hand on her hip, and cocked it to the side, raising her eyebrow. "Let me guess, these must be the Isley Brothers. Let's see here…" she said, tapping her chin. "You are Drew…" she said, pointing to the man with a dark scruff on his face and a beanie on his head. "You are Cade." she said, pointing to the wavy-haired brother. "You are Walker…" she added, gesturing to the one with the large blue eyes "…and you are the youngest, Owen." she said, turning to the floppy-haired brother.

"Wow, beautiful and smart." Drew said, slapping Jaxon on the back before turning his gaze to Dee and asking, "What are you doing with this lug nut?"

Jaxon gave him a "back off" glare, strode over to Dee and possessively pulled her into his side. "She has good taste," he replied, flipping Drew the bird.

"Boys. Keep the profanities to a minimum, tonight please." Rose requested as she put her arm around Dee and guided her up the stairs of the porch, explaining as they went. "My boys haven't all been home for a while, so this is just their strange way of telling each other how much they love each other."

The brothers following behind them echoed her words "I love you" to each other in teasing, taunting voices. Dee couldn't help but shake her head and laugh. *Can't say Jaxon didn't warn me.*

* * *

THROUGHOUT DINNER JAXON couldn't take his eyes off Dee. Seeing her reaction to his crazy brothers, listening to the way she answered all his parents' questions about her family and how she was so unapologetically herself around them, made him overflow with happiness that she was his girlfriend. Looking at his parents and brothers, he could see they were as charmed by her as he was. She had an innate way about her. An ability to bring warmth and joy to every room, and he could tell his parents were impressed. Excusing himself to go to the kitchen to help his mother prepare and serve the dessert, she grabbed his arm and squeezed it, offering him a wide smile.

"Jax, I like Dee very much. She is such a beautiful girl both inside and out and her energy is contagious." his mother beamed as she met his gaze. "I can see how happy she's making you."

Jaxon met his mother's loving gaze and brought her in for a hug, squeezing her tight. Jaxon had always been close to his mother, and she was always his biggest champion. "She makes me hopeful for the future," he confessed.

"You're in love with her, aren't you?" she asked, her eyes searching his and face brightening with the question.

His heart swelled with her question, and he took a deep breath, letting it out slowly, knowing the jig was up. There was no use denying it, especially to his mother. "I am Mom. I love her so much." He admitted for the first time, not just to her, but to himself. "I feel like she's healing my heart."

His mother wrapped him up in another hug, and he could feel her sigh with emotion as she held him. Pulling away, she looked up at him, her eyes glistening with unshed tears as she cupped his face with affection and said, "Oh, my sweet Jax. When your marriage ended, I saw how deeply hurt and broken you were. I hoped and prayed you would one day find someone that could pick up all those shattered pieces and put you back together. I prayed you would find someone that loved you as much as you loved them, and looking at the two of you tonight, I can see Dee has done that. I truly believe Dee is the answer to my prayers for you."

Jaxon's heart felt two sizes bigger with her words, as a feeling of nurturing love radiating from his mother. After his messy divorce and subsequent return to Primrose, he moved back into their house as he tried to figure out what to do next with his life. Having to move back into his childhood home in his 30s wasn't something he was proud of. However, the time of transition back in Primrose and the safe haven of his family home, was what helped him start to pick up the pieces of his life. He was forever grateful to his parents for giving him that time and for surrounding him with support and their unconditional love.

The sound of Dee's raspy laugh, followed by his father's rich, bountiful boom and a collective groan from his brothers broke Jaxon and his mother out of their reverie.

"Pretty sure, Dad is telling his corny Dad jokes again." Jaxon said with a shake of his head and a little chuckle.

His mother rolled her eyes. "Better them than me.

After over 50 years with that man, I've heard more than my share."

Jaxon grinned. If he had half the relationship his parents had in the future, he was certain he would have a truly happy life.

* * *

AFTER DESSERT and more lively conversation, Jaxon leaned in, whispering in Dee's ear. "Would you like to see my old bedroom?"

Dee raised her eyebrows and licked her lips as she asked, "Are you allowed to take a girl up there?"

"We'll find out," he replied, rising from the table, and reaching for her hand as everyone's heads turned to them. "I'm going to give Dee a tour of the house." Jaxon declared to the entire table before he led her away and towards the stairs.

Cade shouted after them, "Better keep your bedroom door open!"

"No hanky panky!" Walker shouted.

Dee laughed as she wrapped her arm around Jaxon, and he guided her up the stairs into the last room along a long corridor. Flipping the lights on, she entered, taking in his childhood bedroom, her gaze sparkling with playful curiosity. Jaxon watched as she ran her hands over his wooden desk by the window, perused a tall bookshelf of trophies and sports awards and checked out a cork board with candid pictures of a younger Jaxon with all his brothers and childhood friends.

"Is this Hayden?" she asked, pointing to a picture of

two teen boys in baseball uniforms sitting next to each other in a dug out.

"It is," he replied to her with a nostalgic twinkle in his eyes. "Hayden and I played baseball together for years. Those were some good memories."

Dee glanced at him, compassion in her gaze, as she observed. "I can see you miss it."

"Yeah, sometimes. I do miss the thrill of the game and the cheering of the crowd. It was exhilarating," he confessed.

"Just like the thrill I get during and after a performance. Nothing better than taking your final bow and hearing the applause." She mused.

Jaxon smiled at the similarities. He and Dee were so completely different, her city and him all country. She is outgoing, bubbly, and excitable. He laid back, calm and quiet. Yet, when it came to their passions, they both enjoyed the adoration.

"I guess we have something in common, then." He added with a grin.

"I guess we do." She replied, squeezing his shoulder as she returned her gaze to his bulletin board and over to a framed picture of him and his mom. "Momma's boy," she commented as she ran her fingers over it and smiled. "Your Mom is awesome."

"She really likes you. She said she could see how happy you make me." he shared sliding his hand around her waist.

Dee settled her head against his chest and grinned as she took in the two posters above his bed, one of Alex Rodriquez and one of Janet Jackson. Dee let out a laugh, taking in the large poster of Janet Jackson in all her vixen glory from her "Love Will Never Do" video. She gestured to the poster and, with a naughty grin, commented, "I see you have a type."

Jaxon reciprocated her laugh and pulled her into him, "I guess I do," he said, leaning in and trailing wet kisses down her neck before he came back up and grazed her earlobe with his teeth.

She leaned back into him more, let out a breathy moan and brought her arm over her head, hooking it around his neck and raking her fingers through his hair. He slid his large hand down her body, lifting her shirt and cupping her breast, teasing its sensitive peak through her lace bra. "Jaxon." she rasped on another moan as he continued to kiss and tease her neck and shoulder. "Lock the door, please."

Jaxon stepped away, went to the door, and turned the lock, then stalked over to her, swooping her into his arms and making her squeal with delight. Laying her out on the bed, he slid his long lean body over her, the charge between them surging as he brought his hands to her face and brushed his lips to hers tenderly. He stared into her gorgeous midnight eyes, his heart feeling like it may burst. He uttered those three words he never thought he would say to a woman again. "I love you."

Dee visibly melted at his declaration and looked into his eyes dreamily, a sweet smile tugging at her lips as she replied, "I love you too J." Overwhelmed with warmth and happiness, he kissed her tenderly, wanting to savor the sweetness of her and the love that surrounded them. Face bright and beautiful, Dee pulled her lips away as she threw her hands above her head, let out an exasperated exhale and rasped out dramatically, "Finally!"

This woman. A deep rumble of a laugh burst from his throat as he asked, "Have you been waiting?"

"Yes!" she exclaimed, giving him a playful slap to the chest. "I didn't want to rush you, but if you haven't figured it out yet, patience is not one of my virtues."

"Oh, I've noticed," he replied as she wrapped her legs around his waist and hooked her ankles around his back as he rocked his thickening arousal against her core. "Now I want to fulfill my teenage fantasy of making out with a beautiful girl in my bedroom."

"Then you better get to it, Cowboy."

CHAPTER 9

One month was all it took for Dee to fall helplessly, deliriously in love with Jaxon. The kind of love they write about in Jane Austen novels; the kind of love old crooners sing about and the kind of epic love you see in old movies. Dee had always hoped one day she would find her person, but she never expected to find him in a small unassuming town like Primrose. Coming off another incredible weekend, she floated into the school ready for another amazing day of rehearsals.

"Ms. Jones!" one of her drama students exclaimed, running up to her with a frantic look on her face. "Someone vandalized our sets."

Dee's smile dropped and her pulse quickened as she followed the student into the gym, only to find the walls of the sets Jaxon had built toppled in a broken heap on the gym floor. The main walls had been bashed in, pieces of particle board broken and strewn around the space. Dee shook her head in disbelief. "Who would do this?" she asked incredulously, her voice cracking with the question.

The principal and a few teachers gathered around the torn apart sets: their shock and dismay clear as they took in the disastrous scene. A group of her students appeared with sad, downtrodden looks on their faces and brooms in their hands as they swept up the strewn about shavings and pieces.

"We're going to figure out who did this, Dee." Mr. Parker, the Principal of Primrose High said, placing a comforting hand on her shoulder. "I already called our security company and am having them look through the security tapes to see if they can identify the culprit."

"Thanks." she managed, stinging tears pricking her eyes. Garrett came to her side and put his arm around her, and she blinked, trying to keep the tears at bay, but it was no use. A few tears escaped as she leaned into Garrett and watched as her students and some of the teachers passed around garbage bags to start the cleanup. Wiping at the wetness on her face, she turned, catching Anders standing in the doorway of his office. He had a satisfied smirk on his face and his large arms were folded as usual over his chest. When he caught her eye, he smiled wide. No show of sympathy or compassion as he simply turned and went into his office. An uneasy feeling settled in her stomach. Her gut telling her that Anders had something to do with this.

Later that afternoon, the principal got back to her with bad news, saying the cameras in the gym had been tampered with so they couldn't identify the vandal. Dee knew in her gut that Anders was responsible. He had been opposing the production from day one and when she refused to go out with him; he had taken things to the next level with his relentless rude commentary, harassment of her team and intimidation, always walking the line of what was appropriate and what wasn't. *But how do I prove it?* Dee wouldn't let one jerk ruin her production and all the hard work she, her dream team, and her students had put into it. *I need to get some advice as to what to do next and what course to take, and it needs to be someone I can trust.*

The door to her classroom opened, and she glanced up from her desk. "How are you doing, Dee?" Garrett asked, entering the drama room, his eyes full of compassion and concern.

"I've been better." She answered honestly, feigning him a smile. "I really need to talk to you, though. I'm not quite sure what to do."

Garrett took a seat on the choir bleacher and Dee rose from her desk and strode over, taking a seat next to him.

"I think I know who vandalized the sets." She shared, meeting Garrett's expectant gaze. "The problem is, I don't have concrete proof."

"Who do you think it is?" Garrett asked, his brows furrowing with the question.

"Anders." she replied with a sigh. "Garrett, I know in my gut it's him. He has been protesting this production from day one, he's constantly hovering over practices, making rude comments to myself, Oliver, and Emersyn, that teeter on the line and then there have been all the inappropriate things he has said to me in the past."

"What kinds of things?" Garrett asked, furrowing his brows.

"When I started here, it was pretty innocent, just some

light flirting and the odd innuendo. Then he started asking me out, persistently, every week. I kept turning him down and, finally annoyed by his advances, I told him I was seeing someone. He seemed ticked off and started prying as to who I was dating." Dee continued. "This was right around when Jaxon and I started seeing each other and, after that, he would bring Jaxon into conversation, attacking him. Really underhanded low blow kind of stuff."

"Did he ever try to get physical with you?" Garrett asked, back stiffening and eyes searching hers. "I'm sorry I need to ask this."

"No, not really. I mean, he would get in my space, always bordering on inappropriate, but he never quite crossed the line. He did the same thing to Emersyn too and made rude comments to Oliver."

Garrett let out a long exhale, ran his hand through his hair, and straightened out his glasses as he replied. "I think you need to talk to the administration and tell them everything you just told me," he suggested, concern in his voice. "I know you're a tough, independent woman and probably felt like you can handle things yourself, but you should've come to me sooner about this. I will always have your back, Dee."

"I know." She answered, looking down at her hands. "I just never thought anyone would do such a thing.

Garrett put his arm around her shoulders and gave it a squeeze. "If you feel he's responsible for the ruined sets, you need to speak up. Not just for yourself, but for your hardworking students and everyone that has helped you put this production together." He said, meeting her gaze with brotherly compassion. "I'm going to be right by your side and we can go in together to speak to the administration tomorrow morning."

Dee gave Garrett an appreciative smile. He was right. She needed to put a stop to this once and for all. *But how will I prove that he's responsible? How am I going to convince the administration that he was the one who destroyed those sets without the security footage?* There were too many questions running through her head and the tension of the day made her head ache and body sag with defeat. *What am I going to do?*

The drama room door opened, breaking Dee from her raging storm of unanswered questions in her head. A stampede of familiar faces entered the room. Jaxon, Davis, Hayden, Ben, Steve, Rami, Savanah, Emersyn, Oliver, Cade, and Owen all entered the room carrying different tools and supplies, looking like a ragtag team on a home improvement show. Dee stood up to face them, a look of puzzled surprise on her face as her eyes flitted between each one.

"I called in the troops." Garrett said with a determined smile. "With Jaxon's help, of course."

Dee looked up at Garrett and over to Jaxon, meeting his concerned gaze. As she looked into his eyes, pure love and compassion shone back at her as all the disappointment, frustration, and sadness of the day rose back to the surface. With tears brimming, she ran into Jaxon's arms and let go, hot stinging tears spilling on his chest as her body shook with sobs. Jaxon wrapped her up in his protective embrace and stroked her hair as everyone gathered around her supportively, their murmurs of consolation filling the room with words of support and encouragement.

"We're going to rebuild these sets and make them even better." Hayden declared with determination. Everyone cheered in agreement as they charged like a stampede down the steps into the gym, with Hayden leading the way.

Davis hung back, his expression one of kindness. "This is how we roll in, Primrose. We step up and help each other. We got you, Dee." he added as he patted her shoulder in reassurance and followed the rest of the crew into the gym.

Dee buried her head back into Jaxon's chest, letting his warmth and comforting scent soothe her. He kissed her head sweetly as he lifted her chin, pinning her with his stare.

"We're going to fix this, Dee. It's all going to be okay," he assured, leaning down to gently brush his lips to hers before pulling her deeper into his protective embrace.

A commotion sounded from the gym and Dee lifted her head, her eyes darting up to meet Jaxon's as shouts followed, causing them to break apart, Dee sprinting down the stairs to the gym with Jaxon hot on her tail.

"This is my gym, and you don't have a right to be in it. This fucking musical is stupid anyways, so get out of here before I go to administration." Anders yelled, his face red with anger and his eyes glaring at the group.

Dee stormed past her crew of friends and stalked over to Anders, but Jaxon caught her arm before she got up in Anders face. Jaxon stepped in front of her protectively, his face inches from Anders, but hands fisted at his sides. "We have every right to be here," he informed in a low, calm voice.

"The hell you do." Anders scoffed. "This is outside the agreed upon time for this idiotic production. Without your sets, this whole thing is done anyways."

"We're here to rebuild them." Hayden informed, stepping up and flagging Jaxon as he narrowed his eyes at Anders in challenge.

Anders let out a huge guffaw. "Rebuild them? Fantastic, more batting practice for me," he mocked, swinging his arms, mimicking swinging a bat as he got up in Jaxon's face and seethed, teeth gritted, voice derisive. "At least one of us can still hit a target. Poor ex-baseball player, never quite good enough for the big leagues," he taunted, before throwing his head back in an unhinged laugh.

Hayden, Ben, Cade, and Davis all pressed forward, ready to step in if needed. Anders, seeing this, took a step back but didn't relent as he glared at them with an arrogant amused look on his face.

"Needed to bring out your army, I see," he boomed sardonically, the first glimmer of apprehension in his gaze as he looked over the four large men glaring at him. "Can't fight your own battles, old man?" He laughed wickedly as he scoffed. "I don't know why you bother with Dee; she'll open those pretty legs for anyone."

"Whoa, that's way over the line!" Garrett exclaimed, everyone's gazes going over to him, standing in the corner with his cell phone up, recording everything. "And I believe Principal Parker will agree with me, Anders."

Anders' face turned beet red with anger as he

screamed and pointed at Garrett. "That's entrapment! You can't record me without my permission. That's illegal!"

"Actually, he can." Cade informed, stepping forward, pulling out his badge from his back pocket as he flipped it open and held it out to Anders. "I'm an RCMP officer, and he's well within his rights under the Canadian Evidence Act."

All color drained from Anders' face as Cade stepped forward and pulled out his cell phone, calmly dialing and putting it to his ear. "Hey, can I get back up? Yeah…Primrose High. I have a suspected vandal in custody. Send a cruiser. I'll bring him in for questioning. See you in 20." Hanging up his phone, Cade returned his gaze to Anders, whose red face had turned so white he looked like he was going to pass out. Cade approached him and clasped his shoulder firmly as he turned him around and said, "Come with me, Mr. Barick. You show me where that bat is, and then you and I are going to take a little drive into the station. I've got some questions for you. Go willingly, and I won't have to use these," he added, pulling out a pair of handcuffs from his jacket pocket and dangling them in the air to show him. Anders' shoulders visibly slumped, and Cade glanced back at everyone, flashing them a smile.

JAXON LET OUT A LONG EXHALE, trying to calm his heart hammering in his chest. Turning around, Dee stood there, her eyes transfixed on Cade and Anders retreating forms, a mix of anger, disgust and utter embarrassment on her face. Her gaze flitted up to Jaxon and immediately glossed over with tears as she pivoted and sprinted back up the gym stairs, disappearing into her classroom. Savanah stepped forward to follow her, but Rami held her back, shaking his head and glancing at Jaxon to go after her instead.

Jaxon entered the drama room, eyes darting around the room, but she wasn't there. Thinking for a moment, his eyes caught on the costume closet door, knowing exactly where she went to hide. Opening the door, the faint sound of crying met him, his heart instantly breaking at the sound.

"Dee?" he asked as he combed through the rows of clothes to find her in the far corner, on the floor, clutching her legs and resting her head on her knees. He approached slowly, and she raised her head, eyes red and her cheeks wet with tears. He slid down next to her and scooped her up, lifting her into his lap. Cradling her, he let her cry, her body shaking as all her frustration came out in a wave of big fat tears. He caressed her cheek with his thumb and swiped at the tears as they fell. Today had been a heavy day for Dee, but it wasn't only the devastating events of this day that were causing this new onslaught of tears. It was the fact that Anders had attacked her integrity and attempted to put seeds of doubt in Jaxon's head regarding their relationship, insinuating that she was no better than his ex-wife. As broken as he had been in the past, never once had he doubted Dee's faithfulness to him, and he needed her to know that he trusted her fully. She clung to him tightly, gripping his shirt as if worried that he may get up and go.

"I'm here Dee, and I'm not going anywhere," he reassured, as she lifted her eyes to meet him. "I know what Anders said about you isn't true. It was just a desperate attempt on his part to not only hurt you but me. Anders is a dick, plain and simple, and not a single person in that gym right now believes a word he said either." Dee swallowed down hard as he continued pinning her in his stare. "I know who you are, and I trust you, Dee. I need you to know I trust you completely and unconditionally. Meeting you and falling in love with you has helped me to heal and trust again."

With midnight eyes so full of love and affection for him, she declared. "I love you Jaxon Isley. I'm wildly, madly, deeply head over heels in love with you."

Jaxon cupped her cheek, his mouth curled into an adoring smile as he leaned in, eyes never leaving hers, their mouths just a breath apart, "I'm head over heels in love with you too." he whispered as he brushed his lips to hers, with sweet tenderness, the pain of the day dissipating and replaced by their love and devotion.

CHAPTER 10

It didn't take long for Anders to confess to destroying the sets, especially when remnants of particle board were found on the bat he kept in his office. He was charged with a misdemeanor for vandalizing school property and his little tantrum, all caught on video by Garrett, resulted in his immediate dismissal from Primrose High School.

With the drama of the past week, the sets rebuilt and only three more weeks of rehearsals left before the dress rehearsal, Dee spent most of her days and evenings working with her cast to tune the fine details. She was so proud of her hardworking students, the support from staff, parents, volunteers, and her dream team to make it all happen. All three shows were sold out and Primrose was vibrating with anticipation of opening night.

Waving to the school secretary as she exited the school, Dee smiled when she saw Jaxon's truck waiting for her in the empty bus loop. Making her way to the truck, she opened the door to be met by Jaxon's megawatt smile.

"Hey there, Beautiful." he said, his deep rich voice instantly warming her from the inside out.

"Hey there Cowboy." she replied, glancing in the backseat, noticing some grocery bags, a pink bakery box and two overnight bags, one of which was from her closet. "What's this?" she asked, eyes full of surprise and curiosity.

"You've been working so hard, and I thought this long weekend we could get away," he said with a hopeful smile. "I hope you don't mind, but I had Savanah raid your closet and pack you a bag for the weekend."

Dee nodded, impressed by his initiative. "I don't mind at all, but where are we going?" she asked, a smile curving on her lips.

"My family has a cabin on the lake," he replied with an excited smile. "It's a really special place for me and I want to take you there. It's a bit of a drive, so I took the liberty of ordering your favorite," he said, reaching behind the seat and pulling out a takeout bag that said Lings Family Restaurant.

She grabbed the bag eagerly and opened it, inhaling deeply as she looked up at Jaxon in question. "Beef and broccoli stir-fry?"

He nodded as Dee beamed brightly at her thoughtful boyfriend and leaned in, brushing a chaste kiss to his lips. "Thank you, J. A weekend away sounds perfect."

* * *

THREE HOURS LATER, they turned onto a gravel road flagged by tall evergreens as it wound through the trees. A large opening appeared, and a beautiful rustic log cabin revealed itself in the clearing. Dee's face brightened as the shimmer of dusk made the lake sparkle in the background. Parking the truck, she got out and surveyed the cabin with wonder and exclaimed excitedly. "This place is amazing!"

Jaxon grinned and reached for her hand. "Let me show you the inside."

Jaxon led her down a stone walkway towards a short, covered porch and the front door. Unlocking the door, Jaxon stepped aside, gesturing for her to enter first. Dee entered, coming into a large entry way as Jaxon hung up the keys and took her hand with a smile. A short hallway opened into a large living room and her eyes widened as she took in the space. The tall ceiling of the cabin was framed with wide log beams. Tucked into the one side was a galley-style kitchen with a butcher block island and five kitchen stools. The kind of kitchen you could see his parents fixing breakfast for their five boys. Dee grinned at the pleasant thought and continued her perusal as she walked deeper into the living room. There was a wooden staircase off to one side, going to the second floor with an overhang where you could see the entire view of the lake through huge floor to ceiling windows. A grand stone fireplace with a large wooden mantel was the focal point of the room, and an oversized long couch with two cozy chairs sat opposite it. Noticing photos displayed on the mantel, Dee walked over curiously. An eclectic array of candid photos stood proudly on display, showing Jaxon and his brothers posing by the lake, pictures of them making silly faces for the camera and all-around having fun. There were pictures of Robert and Rose, both current and past dispersed amongst the candid ones. Dee reached for one photo of them and brought it down to take a closer look. The photo looked old, with sepia shades and muted colors. Robert and Rose smiling brightly, on what appeared to be their wedding day, his young father was tall, dark and dapper in a suit and his beautiful mother looking flawless and elegant in a white lace gown. The photo made Dee's heart swell as she took in their happy, carefree smiles and the beautiful shimmering lake behind them. She glanced out the large windows, the gorgeous background scene the same as the picture. "Were your parents married here?" she asked as Jaxon hovered behind her; his hands on her shoulders and warm breath in her hair.

"They were. My Dad was 20 and my mom was 18," he replied, smiling at the photo. "Just two crazy kids in love."

Dee met his gaze, and she thought her heart may burst from the love she saw there. *Two crazy kids in love*, she repeated in her head. That's exactly what she felt like they were. She sighed at the wistful thought and put the picture back in its place. Sauntering over to the large windows overlooking a deck and the lake beyond, she couldn't imagine a place more serene and perfect. "It is so beautiful here, J."

Jaxon came up behind her, strong arms coming around her body, enveloping her in his warmth as he replied, "My grandfather built this cabin and since then it's been renovated and added onto a few times. The shell is the original cabin, though. I never get tired of the view here. This cabin has so much history and memories for me. This is my happy place."

Dee turned and met his eyes, so contented and happy. She raised to her tiptoes to kiss him, soft and sweet. Pulling away, she said, "I love it here and I love you, J. Thank you for bringing me here."

He took her face tenderly in his hands and brushed his lips to hers again before saying, "Let me bring everything in and you go out onto the deck, sit back and relax."

"Are you sure?" she asked, ready to help him.

"Yes, this weekend is all about you. You go outside, and I'll be with you shortly," he said, leading her to the patio door.

She gave him an appreciative smile and did as he suggested, exiting the cabin onto the deck that overlooked the lake. She walked to the end of the deck, looking out over the spectacular view before her. Tall evergreens framed the lake, casting their mirrored reflections on the water. The sun, still lingering on the horizon, cast the most beautiful glowing hues of golden red, orange, and yellow in the sky. Dee had seen many beautiful Manitoba skies, but this was like nothing else she had ever seen. *This is magical.* As the brightness of the sky was starting to fade, she was so mesmerized by the view that she didn't notice Jaxon behind her until he curled his hands around her waist.

"It's incredible, isn't it?" he mused, his low, rich voice in her ear. "Twilight on the lake is always my favorite."

"I don't think I've ever seen anything like it." she said. "The colors are magnificent."

He pulled her in closer as they stared at the evanescent

light as it slowly faded, and a sea of magnificent stars slowly brightened in the sky.

Dee turned, meeting Jaxon's eyes. "This is exactly what I needed."

Jaxon offered her his handsome smile as he reached up and caressed her cheek. Dee stared up into his loving gaze as the flicker of a flame in her peripheral vision caused her head to turn. Before her was a lit jar candle on an outdoor coffee table and flagging the candle were two glasses of wine and two small plates with a dessert that she couldn't quite make out in the dim light.

"What's all this?" she asked, approaching the table and looking up at Jaxon with wide eyes. "Is this what I think it is?"

"If you're thinking it's the famous Primrose cinnamon bun, you would be right." He chuckled as he took her hand and led her around the coffee table to sit on the outdoor loveseat. "Marnie baked them special for us."

Dee took a seat and Jaxon joined her, reaching for a plush, soft blanket draped over the back of the loveseat as he spread it out over their legs.

"I've heard about this treat. Apparently, according to Savanah, it's orgasmic." Dee shared, wiggling her brows at Jaxon.

A deep rumble of a laugh escaped his mouth as he replied, "I can't speak to that, but I can tell you they are incredible."

Dee cocked a brow at him and playfully swiped her finger through the thick cream cheese frosting on top and held it out to Jaxon. He leaned forward to lick the dollop off her finger and she pulled it away, a coquettish grin on her face as she popped the top button of her blouse.

"Dee, what are you doing?" Jaxon asked, his voice going husky and eyes darkening.

She met his gaze with a wicked grin as she spread the icing down her neck, heading south and dipping into her cleavage.

Jaxon shook his head as a feral growl reverberated from his chest. "You're naughty, Ms. Jones," he scolded as he lowered his head to lick between her breasts, trailing up her neck and meeting her lips with a scorching kiss.

The taste of the rich tangy sweet icing mingled with their kiss as their tongues tangled. Breathless, Dee whispered against his lips. "How about you and I take these to the bedroom?"

Jaxon pulled his lips away, his eyes flashing with desire and a hint of mirth as he gave her a sexy sideway smirk. Flinging the blanket off their legs, Dee couldn't help but laugh at his eagerness as they grabbed their plates and glasses of wine and went inside, climbing the stairs.

A MORNING FOG blanketed the lake as the cool, crisp breeze rustled the evergreen branches surrounding the cabin. Jaxon breathed in deeply, letting the chill of the air rejuvenate his lungs. The smell of pine needles, fresh dirt, dewy grass, and lake water enveloped him, loving how fresh everything was in the morning at the lake house. Sipping from the steaming mug of coffee he held, he thought back to last night and the beautiful woman still asleep upstairs. He grinned, thinking of their naughty food play, which resulted in a very hot, very steamy shower. He thought about how once they were clean; they lay together, relishing the intimacy of staring into each other's eyes as they explored every ridge, contour and swell of their bodies, with their fingertips before they made love, slow and tender. Closing his eyes, he could feel the softness of her skin under his touch and how she responded to him. He could see the love in her eyes as they moved together languidly, taking their time to draw out the pleasure. How she felt beneath him, above him, surrounding and consuming him. All his senses zoned in on her. He had never been with someone like Dee. So passionate, responsive, and so beautiful when she came undone.

He took in another deep cleansing breath as he stared out onto the lake, his thoughts on his relationship with Dee. Every hour, minute and second, he spent with her made him consider more. There was no question he was already committed, and his heart belonged to her. When he considered the future, she was always there. Thoughts of having a family with her God willing, and a beautiful life together, overwhelming his consciousness. Yet not until last night did he even consider that marriage could or should be part of that picture. Even years after his divorce, another marriage was never something that appealed to him, and he had told Dee as much. But as he continued to fall into the chasm of his love for her, and as his heart continued to piece back together, there wasn't even a question that he wanted that ultimate commitment with Dee. Somewhere along the way, between their side-splitting laughter, their late-night talks, passionate intimacy and holding her close to him at night as he listened to her breath, amongst all the wonderful big and small things he had experienced with Dee in the past six weeks, his views had changed. Believing deep down in his soul that Devine Jones was the only woman that could make him believe in the sanctity of marriage again, and that's exactly what she did.

"Good morning, Cowboy." the sweet raspy voice of his love said, breaking him from his thoughts. Her arms curled around his body from behind, the press of her chest against his back and her hands sliding up his torso, making goosebumps rise on his skin. The feel of her hug was so deliciously warm and inviting that he closed his eyes and relished it for a moment. "Thank you for letting me sleep." She cooed, kissing his back and resting her cheek on it with affection. "I didn't realize how incredibly tired I was."

Jaxon turned to face her, planting a kiss on her forehead, before cupping her cheeks and brushing his lips on each temple, each cheek and finally sweeping his lips over hers. Dee beamed, her glowing face, make-up free and natural and her gorgeous braids wrapped up into a colorful scarf. He had never seen anyone more beautiful and radiant in his life. This stunning, ebony woman with the most expressive eyes the color of a midnight sky was his queen, and all he wanted to do was worship her.

She smiled and let out a cute little laugh as she cocked

an eyebrow at him. "You look like you're thinking sexy thoughts, Cowboy. Are you going to share?"

His tongue darted out, moistening his lips as he pressed her into him, her peaked nipples pressing into his hard chest. "How about I show you?"

With his question, he turned, pinning her to the railing, his front to her back. She reached up, hooking her arms around his neck as he kissed down her neck and reached for the hem of her silky chemise nightgown, slowly bringing it up and lifting it over her head. Bare beneath, her skin goose pimpled in the cold lake breeze of the spring morning. Running his hands over her sides, he palmed her breasts, massaging and teasing their stiffened peaks. She moaned as his thumbs taunted the sensitive nubs and he whispered in her ear. "Are you wet for me?"

"Yes." she panted as he continued to caress her breasts and kiss a path down her neck, nipping her shoulder lightly before returning to her ear, his stubble brushing her soft skin, making her tremble as he whispered. "Hold on to the railing and arch your back. I want to take you right here." She complied and gripped the railing tightly as he removed his clothes and smoothed his large hand down the ridge of her spine, taking in the beautiful line of her body and the perfect swell of her behind. The fog started to clear as the sun peeked through the clouds, glimmering off her ebony skin like a spotlight on a stage. With one delicious slide, he buried himself in her molten heat and she cried out, her voice echoing over the lake. He filled her, again and again, setting an unrelenting pace, relishing the exquisite feel of her body pulsing around him, and the gasps and cries of pleasure escaping her lips. Gripping her hips, he took, and she pressed back, meeting him thrust for thrust, the sounds of their skin connecting, drifting on the morning breeze. Dee arched her back, her core pulsing in waves around him as she surrendered to the pleasure with him following closely behind, their names on each other's lips. With aftershocks of their sweet release reverberating through their bodies, Jaxon turned Dee around, pulling her into him and enrobing her in the warmth of his body.

"I want to be like this forever with you, J." she rasped breathlessly as she trembled against his chest.

He sucked in a breath, letting her sweet scent intoxicate him, as a deep yearning bloomed in his chest and his throat tightened with emotion. *I want this forever with you too,* the words on the tip of his tongue yet not able to come out. *I want everything with you,* an unspoken promise lost on his lips as the lingering remnants of fear held on for dear life.

* * *

"HAVE YOU EVER GONE FISHING BEFORE?" Jaxon asked as Dee stepped into the boat, almost losing her balance as she rocked the boat and clumsily took a seat. He handed her a life jacket and put his on as well.

She took the jacket, slipped it on and cocked her eyebrow at him, giving him an "are you kidding me" look as she countered, "Do I look like someone who's been fishing before?"

He surveyed her and replied with a grin, "You are without question the most stylish fisherwoman on this lake." he said with a laugh taking in her wide leg army green pants, yellow low-cut t-shirt, cropped jean jacket, bright yellow rubber boots, Ray Bans and a colorful scarf wrapped around her hair. And of course, now her bright orange life jacket.

"A girl's got to look chic wherever she goes." She said, striking a pose as she lifted her glasses to give him a wink and make him laugh again.

The overcast day had turned warmer as the sun managed to break on and off between the clouds. Jaxon loaded the fishing gear and a cooler into the boat and climbed in too. He started the motorboat, taking them for a ride around the lake, then, finding a good spot in the middle, he cut the motor. The lake was calm, nary a ripple as he opened the tackle box and looked at Dee, who was curiously looking at all the colorful contents. "Which would you like?" he asked. "Pick something that feels lucky."

Dee's eyes sparkled with delight as she perused her options and picked the lure of a rainbow fish. "I think this one will hook me a big one." She said with a smirk.

"Any fin is possible, just don't trout yourself." He deadpanned.

Dee started to laugh, the raspy edge of her voice echoing across the water. "Now that I've met your parents, I can totally see you turning into your dad."

"Yes, we both have very sofishticated senses of humor," he added with a wink.

"Dear Cod, you're making me laugh so hard!" she

guffawed, her arms out and nodding her head, saying, "Check out my fishy pun."

He laughed and added, "It looks like we're piranha roll."

Dee laughed, her jubilant face suddenly turning serious as she glanced over the edge of the boat at the water surrounding them. "We don't have piranhas here, do we?"

Jaxon threw his head back, laughing hysterically, and reached for her knee, squeezing it for reassurance. "No, Dee. No piranhas in Manitoba."

She feigned wiping her brow in relief as she flashed him her adorable, dimpled smile and gave him a playful wink.

Showing her how to attach the hook, he opened the cooler and pulled out a plastic container.

"What's in there?" she asked curiously.

He opened the container to find small cubes of cheese. "This is our bait. This lake has a lot of rainbow trout and, believe it or not, they like cheese, so we are going to see if we can catch our dinner."

Excited to give this a try, Dee baited her hook and let Jaxon show her how to cast her line into the lake. Holding tightly to her pole, he did the same and sat down next to her, slowly reeling in the line.

"Now what?" she asked with a shrug and a laugh.

"Now we wait. Fishing takes a lot of patience. Just keep reeling in slowly, casting back out again and enjoying the scenery. I've always found fishing to be super relaxing."

She sighed, rolled her neck, and relaxed her shoulders

as she slowly reeled in her line. Casting it out again, Jaxon gave her a look of approval, impressed with her quick mastery. She glanced around them, the water shimmering from the afternoon sun trying to sift through the clouds. Everything smelled so earthy and fresh, and she closed her eyes, listening to the sounds of the water rippling lightly, and the unmistakable haunting wail of a loon echoing off in the distance. Opening her eyes, she noticed Jaxon watching her in his peripheral vision with a huge grin on his face.

"It's peaceful here, isn't it?" he asked.

"So peaceful." She agreed with a contented sigh. "This place feels like you." Jaxon gave her a puzzled look, his eyes asking her to elaborate. "You just have a way of bringing calm to every space you're in." She answered. "I'm constantly on the go; my brain never seems to shut off with continuous to do lists checking off as I go. I chronically overthink everything and spend far too much time trying to work through the rushing thoughts in my head. With you, when we're together, all those thoughts are quiet, and you give me a chance to just be still. A much-needed moment of calm."

Jaxon smiled and reached for her hand, lacing his fingers through hers, and leaned in, brushing her lips with a tender kiss. With one hand on the fishing rod, Dee curled her fingers in the soft hair at the nape of his neck, teasing his mouth to open and deepen the kiss. Just as their kiss turned from gentle to passionate, Dee felt the rod she was still gripping start to pull and tug breaking her from their embrace. She grabbed the rod with both hands and shouted, "I think I have a bite!" Jaxon wrapped his arms around her, helping her reel in her catch and as the fish fought and came closer. He grabbed the net, scooped her catch while Dee dropped her rod to the floor of the boat and clapped excitedly while she squealed, "I caught a fish! I caught a fish!"

Jaxon laughed as he unhooked her line and held the fish up for her to see. "You just caught your first rainbow trout! Well done, babe."

Dee beamed with unbridled excitement as Jaxon showed her how to hold it and he took a picture of her, proudly holding up her impressive catch before they set it in the cooler.

With all the excitement, they didn't notice the clouds darkening above them. A few fat drops of rain fell from the sky, and Jaxon glanced at Dee and let out an exasperated laugh. "Rain always seems to find us."

"It does!" she replied, mirroring his laughter as the sky suddenly opened and the rain started to pelt down on them.

Dee squealed as Jaxon scrambled to start the motor of the boat. With the motor fired up they made their way through the pouring rain towards the lake house. He pulled the boat up to the dock, anchored and tethered the boat then disembarked to help Dee climb out after him. Taking her hand, he twirled her around and pulled her flush with his body. She arched her back, spread out her arms, raised her face to the sky, and laughed with so much glee, the sight of her rapture made his smile so wide his face hurt. Dee was everything. She was light. She was joy. She was all things bright and glorious. Completely enraptured by her radiant happiness shining through the blanket of rain, their eyes met, and he could see his entire future reflected in their midnight depths. Cupping her face, they both blinked through the rain as he crushed his lips to hers, kissing her deeply and profoundly, letting the spring rain wash away what was left of his fears as he declared to himself, *I'm going to marry her.*

CHAPTER 11

$\mathcal{E}$ntering the office, Jaxon made his way to his desk and took a seat. Leaning back in his chair, he ran his hands through his hair, his mind full of thoughts about his weekend with Dee, his epiphany and what to do next. Entering the weekend, he thought this getaway would be fun and a little escape for them. A way to spend some time in his favorite place with his favorite girl. What it ended up being was a catalyst for him to tackle his fears about marriage and, as a result, all he could think about was marrying Dee. He had never been so sure about anything in his entire life. What he thought was love before never felt like this, and he knew without a shadow of a doubt that he wanted to spend the rest of his life with her. *But is it too soon? We've been dating for less than 2 months. Is she ready to marry me?* A barrage of questions firing off in his head.

"Hey, Jaxon, how was your weekend away?" Davis asked, coming into his office and setting down a bakery box.

Jaxon offered his friend a wide smile, knowing there was no way to hide his happiness.

Davis laughed in response and answered his own question. "I believe that smile says it all."

Jaxon leaned onto his desk and ran his hand over his chin as he looked up to meet Davis. "When did you know you wanted to marry Marnie?"

Davis sat back in his seat and a nostalgic smile curved his lips as he answered, "Our love story had a lot of twists and turns with me being overseas more than with her for 2 ½ years but if I'm being honest, I knew after our first two weeks together that she was going to be my wife someday. We just had so many factors that extended our trajectory," he answered. "If I was here though and not deployed, I have no doubt we would have been married within months. Are you thinking about asking Dee to marry you?"

"I am," he replied. "I want her to be my wife. She's my person, I have zero doubt on that, and I don't think I've ever loved anyone more than I love her."

"Last time we spoke, you had no idea if getting married again was something you wanted. So, what changed?" Davis asked curiously.

Jaxon laughed and shook his head. "I don't know if I can pinpoint it, to be honest. It's simply her," he said, shaking his head. "She just pieced me back together. She's the one meant for me."

Davis smiled and laughed, nodding his head. "The right girl tends to do that. Sounds like you're ready then, my friend. What's the plan?"

"I don't know, but I need to get her mother's blessing

and I need to make it big," he said. "Dee deserves something as showstopping as she is."

DEE PULLED up to Dex's sporting goods store and got out of her car. With Jaxon having plans today with his brothers, she figured now was as good a time as any to put together a surprise for his birthday. Although they had plans with his family on Sunday, she had him all to herself on Saturday and with Hayden and Davis's help; she had the perfect way to spend the day with her main squeeze and all their friends. Walking into the store, Dex was hunched over the counter with a book in hand. He looked up and smiled as she approached him.

"Why, if it isn't the beautiful Ms. Devine Jones? What brings you to my humble sports shop?" he asked, coming around the counter to greet her. His cheeks dipped into endearing dimples, which made her smile at his warm welcome.

"Saturday is Jaxon's birthday and I have a surprise planned for him. I was wondering if you happened to have a jersey from his Minor League team that he played for and if so, could I get you to put a number on the back for me, along with his name?" she asked curiously.

"Ah yes, the Buffalo Bisons! Will this jersey be for him or for you?" he asked as he made his way across the store, and she followed.

"For me," she answered.

He nodded his head in approval and guided her to a section in the back corner, where he combed through several racks before he pulled a jersey out and held it up to her. "Last one. It's probably a little big for you, but I think it will do."

Dee nodded and beamed with excitement as Dex walked her and the jersey over to the counter.

"Now, what exactly do you want on the jersey?" he asked with a smile. "I could put a number one and Isley on the back."

"Yes, that sounds perfect, Dex. Thank you."

Dex set to work as Dee watched him place the letters on the jersey first.

"So, Ms. Devine Jones, how is your musical coming along? I can't wait to see it. Less than two weeks till curtain call," he said with a smile. "Did you bring my ticket with you?"

"It is going fantastic and yes, I did!" she exclaimed, reaching into her purse, and pulling out the ticket, then handing it to him. "Here you go."

He held up the ticket and smiled. "Ah, the theatre. I do miss it sometimes. It used to be such a big part of my life, but 27 years ago I bought this place and, well, I guess I never looked back."

Dee leaned on the front counter, finding Dex fascinating and wanting to know more, she asked, "Why did you walk away from it? Perhaps you could have continued even on a smaller stage. Maybe community theatre."

"Yes, I thought of that, but honestly, after doing *Dream Girls* and losing the love of my life, I just didn't have the heart for it anymore," he confessed.

Dee brought her hand to her heart and her brows

drew together in sympathy for this sweet man. "Oh, I'm so sorry, Dex. How did she pass?"

"No, no, she didn't pass away, at least I hope not, but she did sort of disappear on me. I found out she moved away, and I was never able to locate her. I tried, trust me, but it was like she had vanished," he said with a look of melancholy on his face. "I still think of her all the time, though. She was so incredibly beautiful. We were both in the *Dream Girls* cast with me playing Curtis and her Effie. Goodness, I can still hear her singing, "And I Am Telling You I'm Not Going". Her voice was so powerful." He stood there lost in thought for a moment and shook his head. "That was so long ago now, but funny how the heart never really forgets."

Dee's mind wandered to when she was younger, and her mother would play the soundtrack for her. Loretta Devine would belt out the song and her mother would sing along, expertly capturing each gorgeous note and telling her that Effie was her favorite role. At that lovely childhood memory, Dee blinked, once, twice, three times, a spark of realization hitting her square in the face. She stood up straight, hands gripping the counter and knuckles turning white as her eyes darted over to Dex as he positioned the number and pressed the iron down on the jersey, sealing it to the fabric. He caught her stare in his peripheral and turned his head to smile at her, his cheeks dipping into dimples. Dee instinctively touched her face, feeling the dip of her dimples too and her eyes widened as she asked, "What year did you star in *Dream Girls?*"

"1997" he said wistfully. With his answer, Dee knew. She was talking with her father.

* * *

THE ENTIRE WAY home from Winnipeg, Dee's head was a tornado of swirling thoughts and revelations. Dexter was undoubtedly her father. Everything pointed in that direction, and she wasn't quite sure what to do about it. She had moments in her life when she considered searching for her father, but had never made an actual attempt. Everything her mother told her over the years made her apprehensive. He was presented to her as the bad guy. The man that broke her mother's heart. From what Dex said today, it sounded like it was the other way around. *What am I going to do with this information? Do I confront my mother? Do I tell her I found my dad?* So many questions were racing through her head all at once and she needed to talk them out and figure out her approach to getting the truth. She needed to confide in Jaxon.

Knowing Jaxon would be at her apartment, she entered, her head reeling from the revelation of the day.

"Hey, babe!" he called from the kitchen, the sizzle of the wok and the spicy scent of ginger in the air.

She hung up her jacket and bag and joined him in the kitchen where he was hard at work, chopping vegetables for a stir fry.

"Hey, Cowboy, what's cooking?" she asked with a faint smile as she peeked into the wok and went on her tiptoes to give him a chaste kiss.

"Just a little stir-fry I'm whipping up," he replied as he met her gaze and narrowed his eyes, taking in her mood. "Is something wrong, babe? I'm getting a vibe that something is bothering you."

Dee took a seat at the island and swiped her hand over her face, then sighed. *Might as well dive right in.* "I think I know who my father is."

Jaxon's eyes widened as he slowly blinked at her and asked for clarification. "Did I just hear you correctly?"

"Yeah. I'm freaking out here, Jaxon. Like, seriously freaking out!" she exclaimed, panic edging her voice.

He turned off the burner and came around the island, wrapping his arms around her supportively as he reassured, "It's going to be okay, Dee, I promise you that."

She gripped his arm and sucked in a deep calming breath, letting it out slowly and sighed a loud dramatic sigh.

Jaxon sat down on the stool next to her and turned her swiveling stool to face him, taking her hands in his. "Who do you think your father is?"

"Dex." Jaxon's eyes widened, and he looked to her for an explanation. "I went down to his shop today to drop off his ticket, and we started talking about his time as an actor. He shared with me that the reason he left acting behind was because the love of his life had left him. He said she sort of disappeared and moved away. In his words, she vanished into thin air."

"Wow, that's crazy, but what makes you think that it was your mom?" he asked, his brows knitted together.

"Dex told me he fell in love with his co-star from

Dream Girls, the woman who played Effie. Then I remembered my mom talking about playing that role and when I asked him what year he was in it, and he said 1997, which is the same year my mom was in that musical," she said with one exasperated breath. "I knew immediately. That's the year before I was born. Jaxon, we have the same smile too. We both have dimples, and my mom doesn't have them."

Jaxon shook his head at the situation and ran his hands through his hair, then met Dee's eyes with a question. "How are you going to approach your mom?"

"I honestly don't know. She has been telling me a completely different story my whole life. Always made my dad out to be this bad guy who seduced her, then rejected her and now, according to Dex, she was the one that left him and cut off communication. Someone is not telling me the truth and I think it's my mom. But why would she shut him out, and more importantly, why would she not want him in my life?" she asked, shaking her head. "None of it makes sense to me."

"Well, we have plans to have dinner with her tomorrow night, so it might be a good time to investigate. If it were me, I would approach this one carefully and not tell her everything you know just yet. Especially if you want to get some honest answers," he said, offering his opinion. "There has to be a good reason why she did what she did."

Dee sighed, folding her arms around Jaxon. No matter what way she looked at it, this conversation was going to be a difficult one.

* * *

JAXON PULLED into the driveway of a cute little bungalow in St. Augustine. The house sat on a quiet street in the older part of town, where huge trees lined the street shading each yard. The house was bright blue with yellow trim and looked friendly and vibrant from the curb. Definitely a house to match the personality of Barbara Jones.

Dee knocked on the door with Jaxon standing next to her holding a bouquet of spring flowers. The door flew open, and her mother smiled widely in greeting. Barbara, at the age of 56, was undoubtedly a beautiful older woman. Her salt and pepper hair were braided pristinely, and her natural, make-up-free face was warm and nurturing. She had blessed her daughter with not only her beauty, but her dynamic personality.

"Well, if it isn't my lovely daughter whom I never seem to see anymore and the reason I don't see her," she declared with a wry laugh as she hugged Dee and flashed Jaxon a playful wink.

"Mom, that's no way to greet us," Dee scolded as she moved on to enfold Jaxon in a hug.

"Oh, I'm just joking, Dee! Seriously, just poking a little fun at you two lovebirds." She said with a smile. "C'mon in! Dinner is almost ready."

Dee and Jaxon walked into the front entrance and Barbara lead them straight into the kitchen, the smell of freshly fried chicken permeating the space. Jaxon glanced around the small kitchen and smiled. Her kitchen was cute and cozy with bright yellow cabinets, a little portable butcher block island on wheels that could be tucked into the corner, butcher block countertops and a retro fridge and stove. A round wooden table with four chairs sat in the corner under a portrait of Barbara and a much younger Dee. Everything about the mid-century kitchen was warm and inviting, and Jaxon immediately felt at home.

The table was already set for their dinner, with three place settings: a casserole of mashed potatoes, a bowl of coleslaw, and a basket of buttermilk biscuits. Barbara went back to her stove, the sizzle of hot oil sounding as she picked up a pair of tongs and flipped over pieces of chicken.

"It smells great in here, Barbara. Dee has told me all about your famous fried chicken. I can't wait to try it." Jaxon said with excitement.

"Old family recipe." She replied with a smile as she took the last batch of fried chicken out of the pan and turned off the burner. "Alright, it's ready. Take a seat, kids."

As they sat together enjoying lively conversation, laughter, and delicious comfort food, Jaxon could see the tension in Dee's shoulders, and he supportively placed his hand on her knee under the table. She glanced up at him, a look passing between them, telling him that Dee was trying to find a moment to address what happened with her mother and father. He wasn't sure how or when she would broach the subject, but he was ready to be her wingman when she did.

With Dee completely distracted by her mission

tonight, Jaxon had a mission of his own. All he needed was to get Barbara alone.

"Let me do the dishes." Jaxon said bringing the left-overs to the little island. "It's the least I can do for that delicious meal."

"Oh, Jaxon, you are a gentleman. Your mama taught you right. Thank you." Barbara beamed as she turned to Dee. "I was going to pull out some of your photo albums from the attic, but I hadn't had a chance. Do you think you could go up there and find them? The box should be marked."

"Are you going to subject Jaxon to my baby photos?" Dee asked with a laugh.

"Of course! You were the cutest baby, and a mama needs to brag a bit," she answered, her face bright and happy.

"Okay, come get me in 15 if I don't return. Lots of memories up there." Dee responded her eyes darted to Jaxon, gave him a sly thumbs up and he, nodded knowing she was about to dig for evidence.

Barbara slid up next to him with a dish towel in hand. "Now that my daughter isn't within earshot. I wanted to ask you, what are your intentions with my dear daughter? It seems you two are serious."

Thank you, Barbara! Jaxon internally exclaimed the window of opportunity opening.

"I'm glad you asked," he began, turning and meeting her inquisitive gaze, ready to pour his heart out. "Barbara, your daughter and I love each other very much. She's the most incredible woman I've ever met, and she makes me so very happy. I think I make her happy too. I want to spend the rest of my life with Dee, and I would like your blessing to ask her to marry me. May I have your blessing?" Barbara peered up at him stone-faced, blinking slowly, deliberately, taking in his question, and searching his eyes. Nervously, Jaxon continued, "I'm very aware that our relationship has been a quick one, but I've never felt this way about anyone before. I literally can't imagine my future without her. I want to marry her, create a happy life with her, have children someday, if possible, and cherish her for the rest of our lives."

Barbara's chin started to wobble as Jaxon stared into her now glassy eyes. His own emotions surfaced as he watched her process his words and he touched her shoulder with affection, his words cracking as he added, "I'll love Dee till my last breath, and I promise I'll take care of her."

Barbara blinked, and a tear escaped, which she quickly wiped away as her lips slowly drew up into a watery smile. "Jaxon, you're a good man. I can see how much you love my daughter, and I can see how much she loves you. You undoubtedly make my daughter very happy. Yes, Jaxon, I would be so proud to have you as part of my family. You have my blessing."

Jaxon's heart burst with her words as he pulled Barbara in for a hug, her maternal love surrounding him. As they pulled away from their embrace, her mother took his hands and beamed sure and bright, with so much joy and happiness on her face as she said. "Now tell me how you're planning to ask."

"Well, I was thinking..." he started before Dee came

bounding around the corner with a stack of photo albums in her hands.

"Found them!" she exclaimed cheerily as she looked from Jaxon to her mother, then back to Jaxon and narrowed her eyes at them quizzically. "Did I interrupt something here?"

Barbara, going into full actress mode, replied, "Heaven's no! Just got something in my eye." As she started blinking rapidly and turned, drawing her attention back to the dishes.

Dee gave them a skeptical look, then offered to finish up the dishes with Jaxon, telling her mom to go out to her little sunroom and relax. Once they were alone, Dee looked at Jaxon as she leaned into whisper, "I think I've figured out how to get more information from my mom about my dad."

Jaxon looked at her curiously as she produced a photo from her back pocket and held it out to Jaxon. "Do you see who I see?" she asked, pointing to a man standing next to her mother in the photo.

Jaxon stared at the photo, a younger Dex smiling back at him. His eyes flitted up at Dee, as he replied, "There is no question now, that's definitely Dex."

"I'm right then. Dex is my father, and this is a cast photo my mom had stored away in the attic in a box marked theatre memories." She said determinedly. "I remember my mom having this picture out when I was a kid and every now and then I would find her staring at it and holding it to her chest. This may be the only picture she has of him." She said, turning the photo and smoothing her fingers softly over the image of her mother and Dex. "I'm sure she still loves him; my mom has never moved on with any other man. No boyfriends, no dates that I know of. Nothing. I'm certain because she kept this photo, she still holds a candle for him." Her brows drew together and her voice turned light and airy as she mused, "I can't imagine how lonely she's been all these years and honestly it all makes sense why she was so protective over me."

"You were all she had left of him." Jaxon added, as he shook his head. Suddenly a realization struck him, and his eyes darted to Dee. "Isn't Dex coming to closing night of *Singin' in the Rain?*"

"He is," she replied, meeting Jaxon's eyes as she clasped her hand to her mouth and added. "And my mom is coming to the musical that night, too."

"Looks like we could be looking at a family reunion." Jaxon said, his arms coming around her waist as he met her wary gaze.

"I guess we are."

FINISHING UP THE KITCHEN CLEANUP, Jaxon and Dee found her mother relaxing with her feet up on a chaise in her sunroom off the back of the house. The room was small and cozy, like the rest of the house, with only a wicker loveseat, matching chair and a velvet chaise, which you could tell was her mother's favorite place to read and relax.

Dee had the stack of photo albums in her arms and Jaxon was holding two glasses of wine, one for Barbara and one for Dee. Handing one to Barbara, Jaxon settled in next to Dee as she opened the first album, showing him pictures of her as a baby. Jaxon paged through the album, his smile growing wider with each adorable photo.

"Wasn't Dee the cutest baby?" Barbara cooed. "She has always had a smile that can charm anyone."

"She is and still does." Jaxon replied, meeting Dee's loving gaze and giving her a wink.

Dee turned to her mother, determined to gather more evidence. "Mom, I've always wondered where I got my dimples from, as you don't have them. Did my dad have dimples?" Dee asked, fishing for information and flitting a quick glance to Jaxon, saying 'I'm going in.'

Barbara glanced away, looking distant a moment before returning her gaze to Dee. "Yes, you have your father's dimples." She answered simply.

Dee nodded. *Okay, now to dig deeper.* "I've been thinking a lot about my dad lately, wondering what he's doing now and if I should try to find him. Even if he doesn't want to be a part of my life, it would be nice to just meet him." She declared, as she nonchalantly browsed her childhood photos with Jaxon and purposely avoided looking her mother's way. "I sometimes wonder if he still acts or is involved in theatre. Perhaps he's famous, who knows." Dee chanced a quick glance at her mother, her expression sullen and stoic. *Not even a noticeable flinch. She's a good actress.* "I guess I sometimes wonder why he chose to not be a part of my life. Even if he was just a dad that came around during the holidays and I only saw him occasionally, it would've been nice to have known him." She went on. "It makes me wonder what happened between you two and what caused him to make the choices he made. To cut all ties with you."

Barbara went to speak and closed her mouth, her mind obviously racing from everything Dee was saying to her and not wanting to blow up at her in front of Jaxon. She turned away and cleared her throat then turned back to them, a well-rehearsed smile painted on her face as she replied, "Your father was a very handsome, very talented man and although I have no idea if he continued to act, I'm sure he's made himself a good life. Perhaps he's gotten married and had a family. Perhaps he ended up with someone that his family approved of. Either way, I'm sure he's somewhere and if you insist on finding him, that's up to you." Her voice was steady and resolute.

Bingo! This was the first time her mother gave her any indication that perhaps the reason he wasn't a part of her life wasn't actually his fault. It sounded like it wasn't her fault, either. *It sounds like his family played a part in all of this. But why did they object to them being together?*

"So, you and my dad couldn't be together because of your families? That sounds very Romeo and Juliet." she said, making the connection to the Montagues and Capulets.

Barbara ran her hand over hair and looked away, letting out a dramatic sigh and Dee had her answer. Knowing her mother was finding this conversation difficult, she pulled back and pointed to a picture of her in first grade. "That's me in my first school play," she told Jaxon with a satisfied grin, as he flashed her a knowing smirk. She had the information she needed and as she sat here in her childhood home, reliving memories with her mother and the man she loved at her side, she was struck with one all-consuming thought. *I need to make things right between my parents.* If her parents were victims of their families keeping them apart, then now, 28 years later, there was no reason why they couldn't be together. Even if the spark of love had faded with time, they could without question be a part of each other's lives and hers.

CHAPTER 12

Jaxon woke to the sound of the shower going and rolled over on Dee's side of the bed, still warm from the heat of her body. He lay back and ran his hands through his hair as he stared at the ceiling. Today, he was 38 years old, and as he lay there, the scent of Dee surrounding him, Jaxon reflected on how much his life had changed over the past few months. If you were to ask him, last year at this time, if he would be here, hopelessly in love with the most beautiful, interesting, and dynamic woman he had ever met and planning an epic proposal, he would've simply laughed and scoffed. His life, dare he say his world, was forever changed when he splashed Dee with that puddle. He smiled and laughed internally. *Who would have thought that damn prairie rain would bring us together? Thank you, mother nature.*

The ensuite door opened to a cloud of steam and Dee emerged looking beautifully flushed and sexy in just a towel and her braids pulled back off her fresh natural face.

"Good morning, birthday boy," she said, sauntering over to him, swaying her round hips with each step. Crawling into the bed, her midnight eyes pinned on his, she climbed over him to straddle his hips.

A low, sexy rumble of approval escaped his throat as he took in his ebony vixen and unraveled the towel, tossing it to the floor. He took in every exquisite curve, dip and contour, her body a work of art, and pure perfection in his eyes. "God, you're beautiful." He said, coasting his hands over her curves and settling them on her ample hips.

"And you, Cowboy, are so handsome." She replied, smoothing her hands over his sides. "Did you get sexier overnight or am I just imagining it?" she asked with a coquettish smile as she slid her hands over his chest and up along his stubble jawline before she leaned over and kissed him sensually. His body responded, one touch from Dee making him rock hard and ready. Pulling away from his lips, she cocked an eyebrow at him, the way she always did and asked, "Do you want your first birthday gift now or later?"

"Now." he replied huskily as he pulled her down for another sensual kiss. She peeled away again, climbed off him and let out a raspy laugh. "Hold on there, Cowboy. Let me go get it."

He groaned and reached out for her, trying to grab her as she went and pull her back on top of him. Dee laughed that sexy as sin raspy laugh he adored as she slipped into her walk-in closet and closed the door behind her. Jaxon turned onto his side, propping his head up with his hands as he waited with anticipation. Suddenly the closet doors flew open, Dee emerging in nothing but a Buffalo Bisons jersey. Jaxon's jaw slacked and his arousal grew impossibly harder at the sight of her. She brought her hands to her waist and posed for him, then slowly turned to show him the back. Number one and the name Isley were printed on the back in bold letters. She turned back to face him, and he stared at her, sliding his legs out from under the covers and sitting up.

Staring at him with a look of uncertainty, she asked, "Do you not like it?"

He shook his head and let out an incredulous laugh as he rose from the bed and stalked over to her, lifting her into his arms and cupping her behind. "You are literally one of my fantasies come true."

A coquettish smile curled her lips as he turned and tossed her to the bed, causing her to bounce and let out a delighted squeal. Crawling over her, the heat of his body on top of her and his hips pinning hers to the mattress, she cocked a wicked brow at him and murmured. "Tell me more about these fantasies."

THE SPRING AFTERNOON was sunny and warm, a perfect day to go for a walk as they strolled down the street past the residential area towards the recreation center. Dee, having convinced him to show her where he used to play baseball for Primrose, bounced with barely contained excitement as they walked, Jaxon carrying a wooden bat and Dee with his leather glove and ball. A dozen cars sat in the parking lot as they approached, but thankfully Jaxon paid them no mind as they rounded the back of the recreation center to where the baseball diamonds were. A huge banner that read "Happy Birthday Jaxon" along with bunches of balloons tied to the chain-link fence, greeted them along with all the faces of their friends, and Jaxon's eyes widened with recognition. Davis, Marnie, Hayden, Whitney, Ben, Ever, Garrett, Bea, Rami, Savanah and the Isley Brothers were all there, smiling and dressed to play ball.

Jaxon glanced down at Dee, the biggest smile on his face as he asked. "What's this?"

"It's a birthday baseball game!" she exclaimed as their friends and family approached, clapping Jaxon on the back and giving him hugs as they wished him a happy birthday.

"Are you ready to get your ass kicked, big leaguer?" Hayden taunted as he punched a glove with his fist.

"Hastings, you better watch your mouth as I'm about to hand you your ass," Jaxon volleyed, making him laugh. Jaxon wrapped an arm around Dee and pulled her into him as she raised her chin to meet his ocean blue gaze. "Babe, this is perfect. I love you."

"Love you too," she replied, reaching up and tugging him down for a chaste kiss before pulling away and cocking a brow at him. "Now get that cute ass out there and show me what you got."

To start the game, they gathered near Homeplate to pick teams. With Ever and Marnie, both pregnant and Davis unable to run due to his past military injury, they became the cheering section, so that left everyone else to be picked. With Dee chosen to be on the opposite team as Jaxon, the smack talk began, and she was here for it.

As Dee came up to bat for the first time, she swallowed down her nerves, remembering how Jaxon taught her on their first date. *Eye on the ball and follow through straight.* With Cade pitching to her, she narrowed her eyes at him, giving him a death glare, and he laughed at her attempt at intimidation.

"Don't underestimate my girl!" Jaxon shouted from first base. "She is a solid hitter!" he bragged, flashing her his endearing smile.

Cade pitched one to her and Ben, who was the catcher and umpire, yelled, "Ball!"

"You got the next one, Dee." Ben commented in his deep baritone as he offered her a smile.

Although Ben Hastings was probably the largest, most intimidating man she had ever met, he truly was just a big old teddy bear.

"Thanks Ben." she replied with a smile as she set her stance, positioned her hands, and stared down Cade.

Cade pitched. She swung, just a hair too late.

"Almost had that one, Dee!" Davis yelled from the stands. "Next one's yours!"

Dee looked at Jaxon and he gestured to keep her eye on the ball, then gave her a thumbs up. Taking position next to home plate, she did as Jaxon reminded, eye locked on the ball. Cade pitched and as the ball came towards her, she swung the bat with all that she had and connected, making it fly towards Whitney in centerfield. In complete shock, Dee started jumping up and down with excitement as everyone yelled, "Run, Dee, Run!"

Dee ran to first base, tagged it just as Jaxon caught the throw from Whitney and Ben yelled, "Safe!

Dee squealed with delight and wrapped her arms around Jaxon. "I love baseball!" she exclaimed, pure exhilaration on her face.

God, I love this woman. Jaxon leaned in, his breath hot at her ear as he whispered, his voice a low growl, "I'm so crazy turned on right now."

Dee cocked her brow at him as the memory of their first date passed between them and she hopped into his hold, wrapping her legs around his waist.

"This feels a little Déjà vu," Dee mused before she crushed her lips to his in a deep passionate kiss, her tongue sliding against his deliciously.

"Player misconduct!" Owen shouted from the bench. "Other team is trying to distract our player."

Everyone else hooted and hollered as they embraced, not caring who was watching. Dee pulled her lips away, laughed sexily, and met him with a lustful gaze.

"We better get back to the game," Jaxon suggested, waggling his eyebrows at her. "Great hit, babe!"

Dee grinned with pride, stole one last kiss, and unwrapped herself from Jaxon's body.

"Hey J, I bet that never happened in the big leagues!" Walker shouted from second base with an amused smirk.

Jaxon laughed and shook his head as Dee glanced up at him, pure love, joy, and bursting delight on her face.

* * *

AFTER THE GAME, everyone gathered in the parking lot for a good, old-fashioned tailgate party. Folding tables were laden with salads and snacks while Ben and Hayden set up portable grills to barbecue hotdogs and hamburgers. Beer and coolers were flowing, and Marnie had made him his favorite cake, carrot with heaps of decadent cream cheese frosting. The sun was setting, and raucous laughter and chatter filled the lot as the light of day dimmed. Jaxon nursed a beer as he sat on the tailgate of Hayden's truck, taking in the scene, his belly and heart full. His gaze drifted over to Dee, who was laughing with his old high school friend Bea as well as Ever Hastings. The raspy lit of her voice like music to his ears. Overhearing the conversation, he chuckled to himself as Bea shared a story about their antics while growing up. He glanced from friend to friend, brother to brother, each one of the people here tonight having a history with him. Some long, some short, but each one an important person in his life. Immense gratitude filled his chest. Grateful for his hometown and the people in it. The people were what made this town so special.

"Hey there, J." the unmistakable voice of Bea Baxter sounded beside him as she touched his shoulder. "Mind if I join you."

"Sure," he replied, patting the spot beside him on the tailgate.

She hopped on and settled in, gripping the neck of a cooler and looked out on all the friends that gathered.

"A lot of good people are here tonight." Bea mused with a contented smile. "All people that love and support you."

He nodded, feeling that overwhelming contentment as well. "There really is. Seriously, why wouldn't everyone want to live here?

"I know, right!" Bea exclaimed. "Glad you came back then?"

"Completely." he answered, scanning his friends and family again, then settling his gaze on Dee.

Bea followed his gaze and grinned, then gave him her usual punch on the arm. "I like her. J. Dee is amazing. And moreover, she's really amazing for you."

"She is," he replied, a little chuckle rumbling from his chest. "Meeting her has completely changed my life."

"I can see that. I can see how happy she makes you, and it's good to see you happy again." Bea said wistfully. "When you came back to Primrose, it was painful to see how broken you were, and I know it's been difficult to move on. Maybe you were just waiting for Dee. You're in love with her, aren't you?"

He nodded and turned to Bea, meeting her gaze. "I've never felt like this before. Even when I was with Leah, it never felt like this. Like Dee was made for me and I was made for her." He shared, his eyes drifting back to Dee as he confessed. "I had completely given up on love and resigned myself to the fact that I would be alone for the rest of my life and then she came along and..."

"Things changed." Bea finished. "Love will do that. It will sneak up on you when you least expect it. Or in my case, move in across the street." Bea mused, catching the eye of her husband Garrett and grinning when he flashed her a wink.

"I want to ask Dee to marry me." Jaxon shared, keeping his voice low.

Bea grinned at that and gave him a nudge, whispering back, "You old dog, you. Honestly, I think she's perfect for you, Jaxon. You two are so different, but I think that's a good thing. She brings out the best in you and you bring out the best in her. And it is as plain as day that she loves you too. Savanah has told me Dee has never been like this with anyone else and she has talked to her about wanting to marry you, too."

Jaxon's eyes flitted to Bea at this tidbit of information as he returned his gaze to Dee. *She wants to marry me too.* That was all he needed to hear. A plan in place, her mother's blessing and now confirmation from a reliable source that he and Dee were on the same page. Time to activate his plan. If he was going to pull this off and give Dee the show stopping proposal she deserved, he needed to get to work. But first find the perfect ring.

It was the last full week of rehearsals before *Singin' in the Rain* was to make its debut on the Primrose stage. With Dee staying late at school all week, it was as good a time as any to go ring shopping. At Bea's suggestion, he recruited Garrett to come help him. Now, as he sat there on his apartment terrace holding a beautiful antique art déco style solitaire ring that had all the panache and drama his soon-to-be fiancé possessed, Jaxon was certain he chose well. Hearing the door to the apartment disengage, he quickly tucked the ring back in its box and stuffed it into his pocket. A moment later, Dee appeared at the patio door, her lovely, dimpled smile greeting him.

"There you are, J." she said as she stepped out onto the deck and curled up onto his lap. Planting a chaste kiss on his lips, she cuddled into him and looked out onto the horizon. "This is nice," she sighed.

Jaxon nuzzled his face into her hair and inhaled the sweet scent of her. *I can't wait to spend the rest of my life holding her like this.* The ring burning a hole in his pocket. The desire to ask her now was so overwhelming, he nearly gave in. *Not yet, Jaxon. Soon.* his inner voice reassured. Tamping down the impulse, he smoothed back her braids and met her eyes, sparkling in the dim evening light. He cupped her face and brought her lush lips to his. *I could kiss these lips for the rest of my life, and I will.* Dee reached for him, tangling her fingers in his hair as their kiss deepened until the match of passion ignited between them and blazed brightly. Breathless, Jaxon broke away, his forehead resting on hers as they breathed in the same air. No words of affirmation needing to be said, just a profound knowing that they were it for each other. He turned his gaze, her head finding the crook of his neck as he stroked her hair, and they watched rain clouds off in the distance fade and a vibrant rainbow arch across the prairie sky.

CHAPTER 13

It was dress rehearsal day and Primrose High was humming with excitement. This was her talented cast of students' first chance to show the staff and their peers what they had been working so hard on for the past two months. The gym filled and Dee bustled around backstage, helping wherever she could. Female students decked out in grand flapper style dresses and fake furs, the boys dressed in vested suits and fedoras, everyone looking like they just walked out of the 1940s. Dee couldn't believe how it all came together. With one final encouraging pep talk with her cast behind the curtain, she made her way into the gym and pulled the microphone from the stand as she faced the anxious audience. "Hello everyone!" she announced, the excited murmur and chatter of the students quieting as she continued. "You all have the privilege of being the first in Primrose to see our production of the award-winning musical *Singin' in the Rain*. Your students and classmates have worked tirelessly on this production, and I hope you love it as much as we do. So, without further ado, we present to you, *Singin' in the Rain*."

As she took her seat in the front row next to Emersyn and Oliver, she nodded to Steve at the piano to start as the projection screen came down over the curtain for the opening sequence to start the show. The next two hours were a stage director's dream, from the cable car meet cute to her talented 12th grade Don Lockwood, singing and dancing his heart out in the rain, to his declaration of love as he asked her 12th grade Kathy Seldon not to go and declared her to be his lucky star. Her students put every bit of their heart and soul into their roles. The entire gym echoed with laughter and cheers as they danced and sang. It was everything Dee hoped it would be and more and she couldn't help but beam with pride at her dedicated students.

As the curtain closed on the last number, the gym erupted in cheers as the curtain reopened for the students to take their bows. Bursting with pride, she turned, and her mouth fell open when it wasn't her incredible cast standing there. Jaxon stood alone on the stage with the spotlight poised on his handsome face. Dee's eyes widened as she took him in, dressed smartly in a pair of 1940s pleated pants, short-sleeved button-down shirt, sweater vest and wing tips. He wore a tan fedora, his unruly hair smoothed down and neat. He looked like Gene Kelly, but still like the country boy she loved, and her heart started to beat rapidly against her chest. *Why is he here? What is he doing?*

Jaxon stepped to the microphone, his expression nervous yet assured as he said, "I have a special song. I want to sing for a very special woman. Someone I love very much, and I know was meant for me." With that he started to sing, his rich deep voice sounding melodic and perfect as he sang Gene Kelly's love song, "You Were Meant for Me". Dee had no idea he could sing like that, and her eyes started to tear up as he transfixed her with his steely blue gaze. As he sang the last line, he asked, "Could Ms. Jones please come up to the stage?"

Oliver leaned toward her, his smile wide, and whispered, "You heard the man, go."

Hesitantly, Dee rose from her seat and looked around, all the faces of students smiling at her, some of her fellow teachers holding their hands to their mouths or clutching their chests with tears in their eyes. Dee walked up to the stage, her cast waiting in the wings all grinning at her as she moved past them and slowly walked towards Jaxon, waiting on stage, his ocean blue eyes glimmering under the stage lights and an endearing smile tilted into a knowing smile. She turned to face him, and he took her hand in his as he lowered to one knee and looked up at her with so much adoration and love in his eyes she was sure her heart was about to burst. "Dee, from the moment I splashed you with that puddle two months ago, I knew my life would never be the same. You put so much love and passion into everything you do, including our relationship, and I want to spend the rest of my life giving you that in return. Dee Jones, you, and I were meant to be. I know it, you know it and mother nature knew on the day we met. I love you so much. Will you marry me?" With his question, he let go of her hand and pulled out a ring box, opening it for her. Inside was a gorgeous antique diamond solitaire, the most stunning ring she had ever laid eyes on.

She looked from the ring to Jaxon's beautiful blue eyes and every smile, every laugh, every touch, every kiss and every intimate moment they shared over the past two months played back like a movie reel. Jaxon Isley was the love of her life, and she wanted nothing more than to spend the rest of her life by his side. "YES!" she exclaimed, loud enough for the entire gym to hear. "YES, I will marry you!"

The gym erupted into a standing ovation as everyone rose to their feet, clapped and cheered. Jaxon looked up at Dee, reached for her hand, and slipped the ring on her finger. With tears brimming she cupped his face and leaned down, brushing her lips to his, soft and sweet, not caring that the entire school was watching.

* * *

WRAPPING his arms around his fiancé, their bodies hot and slick with sweat from their vigorous lovemaking, he pulled the covers over them as he relished the feel of her warm soft skin against his own. Both catching their breath as they held onto each other satiated and spent, Dee asked, "Did tonight actually happen?"

"The sex? Because I can remind you how real that just was." he chuckled, kissing her hair.

She tickled his sides, making him writhe and flip them over, settling between her legs as he pinned her arms above her head and kissed her passionately. She smiled against his lips, and when he pulled away, letting go of her hands, she smoothed the hair out of his eyes, running her hands through his soft hair and giving it a tug. "I meant…" she continued, rolling her eyes dramatically. "…you asking me to marry you in front of the entire school? That was some serious old Hollywood kind of stuff."

"Anything for you, babe," he replied, looking justifiably proud of himself.

"It was perfect." She added, smoothing her fingers over his handsome face. "I can't wait to be your wife and, to be honest, I don't care where or when. I've never had fantasies of a huge wedding."

"How about we get through this week and decide then? Besides, we still need to tell our families and we better do it tonight because half of Primrose knows already, and I'm sure the gossip mill will get to my mom soon," he said with a knowing chuckle.

"Before we do, how about you remind me of what I have to look forward to for the rest of my life." she said, coquettishly raising an eyebrow and wrapping her legs around his back, her hips seeking as he hardened between them.

"With pleasure, future Mrs. Isley."

From opening night till the last night of the show, Singin' in the Rain was declared a hit and everyone around town was talking about it. Between the musical and Jaxon's epic grand gesture of a proposal on stage, tongues were wagging everywhere. Once they told his parents and Dee had called her mom who informed her that Jaxon had asked for her blessing, the video of the proposal taken by Garrett no less was passed around to everyone they knew. Jaxon and Dee were without question the talk of the town.

With tonight being the last night of the show, all their friends and family had their tickets, and the excitement was palpable. Dee pulled out a gold dress she had Savanah curate for her and held it out, admiring the shimmer of the material. When she had tried it on, she instantly fell in love with how it made her feel like an old Hollywood starlet. After all, this to her was like her Oscars and after everything that had happened in the past two months, she deserved to look like a million bucks. Dee slipped out of her robe and stepped into the dress, slipping into it and reaching behind her to zip it up. The bedroom door opened and immediately Jaxon's warm hands were there, slowly sliding up the zipper, making her skin sizzle from the gentle touch of his fingertips. She turned and smiled at him, his blue eyes dancing.

"You are a knockout." He said, taking her in and making her twirl with his hand. "Wow, just wow."

"You don't look half bad yourself, Cowboy." she said, smoothing her hands over the labels of his tailored suit and white shirt casually unbuttoned at the top. "This is a nice look on you, but I think I still like you best in a pair of jeans, t-shirt and a baseball cap."

"And I like you in just a baseball jersey," he volleyed, waggling his eyebrows at her.

"Not appropriate for tonight, but later, perhaps," she answered with a playful wink. "So, afterwards, your parents are hosting a cast party for the students, parents, volunteers and all our friends?"

He nodded, "They insisted. I honestly don't have all the details, but they've set up a tent and Mom has all the Auxiliary ladies baking up a storm. I think they're just excited about our engagement and the final night of the musical gives them another excuse to celebrate," he answered as he watched her reach into a jewelry box on her dresser and pull out some chandelier earrings.

"I think so too. My mom is coming tonight and Dex and all our..." Dee stopped and turned to Jaxon, a wary look on her face. "Dex is going to be there tonight. With all the excitement from this week, I completely forgot."

Jaxon ran his hand through his facial scruff and shook his head before he met her apprehensive gaze and replied. "Like it or not, things are about to get interesting."

Jaxon and Dee arrived at the school early, Dee ducking into the back to check on the volunteers and her students. After they were reminded that Dex was indeed coming to the performance tonight, they decided not to worry and just let things unfold as they will. With Dee having responsibilities backstage, and with Dex being Jaxon's friend, he tried to mentally prepare himself to take on the reintroductions.

Barbara found him quickly, her smile beaming brightly when she saw him. "Well, if it isn't my future son-in-law. Oh, you dear boy! I watched the video you sent me, and it was beautiful!" she cooed, leaning in and giving him a kiss on the cheek.

Robert and Rose Isley appeared through the buzzing crowd and spotted Jaxon. "Jaxon, sweetheart!" his mother exclaimed as she wrapped her arms around him for a hug. His father did the same, and they both looked to Barbara, waiting for an introduction.

"Mom, Dad, this is Barbara Jones, Dee's mother," he said. "And Barbara, these are my parents, Robert and Rose Isley."

His mother and Barbara immediately embraced, making his heart burst as Barbara moved on to his father, giving him a friendly hug as well. Their mothers wasted no time starting a conversation, talking about Jaxon and Dee and their engagement. Within a minute, his mother and Barbara were laughing and chattering like old friends while Jaxon's dad stood next to him, his hands in his pockets, smiling from ear to ear. Jaxon caught his father's grin in his peripheral and turned, meeting his gaze.

"I'm happy for you, son," he said simply. "Dee is truly wonderful, and we're excited to have her as a daughter."

A tightness of emotion rose in Jaxon's chest as he swallowed down to try to keep it at bay. He and his dad shared many of the same personality traits and for his dad to express this much to him about his relationship with Dee meant everything.

Friends, family, and the community of Primrose shuffled into the lobby of the school, many stopping to congratulate Jaxon or wave as they passed. As everyone started moving into the gymnasium, Jaxon spotted Dex, who offered him a wave. *Here we go.* Turning, poised and ready to make introductions, he noticed Barbara and his mother disappearing through the gym entrance, so he had a little more time to figure out how he was going to initiate this. Dex managed to make his way through the swarm of people to Jaxon, greeting him with a firm handshake, and turning to his father, greeting him as well. As the men conversed and the line to get into the gym moved along, it gave Jaxon time to think about how to go about this. There was no perfect way to reacquaint them, so in the time it took to get into the gym he opted to simply make the introductions and hope. Between the audience present and the significance of this night neither would choose to make a scene. As they entered the gym, they were handed programs, and he spotted his mother waving them over to the front. His heart jackhammered in his chest at the anticipation of this reunion as they made their way down the aisle to the front row. When they got there, his mother patted the seat next to her for his father and his mother, friendly as she always was, smiled up at Dex. "Who is this?" she asked.

With her question, Barbara, who had been leaning over and talking to Oliver, turned and her face fell as if she had been slapped in the face by her past. Dex's eyebrows raised in recognition. Jaxon tried to be casual, but all that kept going through his head was *Dee was right. Dex is her father.* Answering his mother, he turned to her, smiled, and as he was about to open his mouth, Dex chimed in.

"Nice to meet you, I'm Dexter Geoffrey the Third. You must be Jaxon's mother, Rose. I've heard so many wonderful things about you from your son and husband," he said, shaking her hand.

Jaxon turned his gaze to Barbara, who looked like she had seen a ghost, and started introductions, "Barbara, this is my friend Dexter Geoffrey. Dex, this is Dee's mother Barbara Jones."

With his introduction, Dex's brows furrowed as his eyes clouded over like he was deep in thought. Suddenly his eyes widened and flitted to Barbara, meeting her stunned and terrified gaze that was glossing over with tears. His gaze softened and his expressive eyes welled with emotion as Jaxon witnessed the silent question that passed between these two star-crossed lovers. Barbara blinked, a single tear cascading down her lovely face as she nodded, confirming his suspicions. Dex swiped his eyes and he cleared his throat to steady himself as he gestured to the seat next to Barbara. She nodded, and he took a seat next to her, putting his hand out to his long-lost love and saying. "It's so wonderful to see you again, Barbara."

Barbara laced her fingers with Dex's, and the look they gave each other was one Jaxon would never forget. The look of two people, still holding on to feelings for each other even though so much time had passed. Letting out the breath he had been holding, Jaxon took his seat in front and center just as Dee appeared from the side of the stage. She looked like a vision in sparkling gold as she gave him a wink and flashed him her gorgeous, dimpled smile. Taking in all the faces of their loved ones in the front row, her eyes settled on her mother and Dex and their joined hands. Her eyes darted to Jaxon, and she gave him a look, saying, "Am I seeing what I think I'm seeing?". Jaxon nodded and let out a little chuckle as Dee reached for the microphone.

"Welcome friends, family and the community of Primrose!" The gym erupted into cheers. "I'm Devine Jones and if you haven't heard yet, soon to be Mrs. Isley." she said, holding up her hand with the beautiful engagement ring and wiggling her fingers. The audience cheered again, a few familiar whoops sounding from the back from some of their friends. She let out her cute, raspy laugh and continued. "For those that don't know, I'm also the drama teacher and Creative Director of the Arts department here at Primrose High and I had the honor of filling the illustrious shoes of Mrs. Doris Newman after 30 incredible years!" Mrs. Newman, also in the front row, stood up and everyone clapped and cheered. She turned to Dee, offering her an approving nod as Dee smiled at her and continued. "Two months ago, I presented this musical to my incredibly talented students, and they have embraced it with so much enthusiasm and passion it has astounded me. They've worked so hard, and that is a testament to the examples of the work ethic in this room. Thank you for supporting them and thank you for supporting this Primrose High tradition." She said with appreciation, as she nodded to Steve at the piano and waved her hand in grandiose fashion to the closed curtain. "Without further ado, it is my honor to present to you the award-winning musical, *Singin' in the Rain!*"

Dee took her seat next to Jaxon and reached for his hand, intertwining her fingers with his, giving him a squeeze as the lights in the gym dimmed and the large screen came down over the curtain for the opening sequence. The piano, along with the opening video, started to play, and Dee leaned into Jaxon, her mouth at his ear. "Thank you."

He met her midnight gaze, so full of love and gratitude, and leaned in, kissing her chastely before they both turned, bringing their attention back to the intro of the musical.

For two incredible hours they were pulled into 1940s Hollywood as the students sang, danced, and acted, leaving their hearts and souls out on that stage. The audience laughed as two boys sang "Moses Supposes" and danced to a number that could rival Gene Kelly himself. They swooned when the pretty girl playing Kathy Selden stood on a ladder as the boy playing Don Lockwood serenaded her. Everyone sang along as three very talented kids sang "Good Morning" and when the *Singin' in the Rain* number started, you could literally hear the collective sigh of happiness from the audience. The entire night was magical, and Jaxon couldn't be prouder of the crazy talented students as well as his beautiful fiancé. Dee had dreamed of bringing this musical to life and she had done it with all the panache and flair that only she could bring.

The curtain came down, and the audience rose to their feet as the gymnasium exploded with loud applause, cheers, and whistles. Dee looked at Jaxon, with happy tears brimming in her eyes as he wrapped her up in a hug and wiped a tear that was rolling down her cheek. "You did it, babe! You did it!" he exclaimed over the cheers of the crowd and Dee grinned, swiping at another tear that managed to escape. She stepped away from their embrace and slipped through the backstage door as the curtain opened and the incredible cast of students took turns taking their bows. The standing ovation continued, and the crowd erupted again with a swell of applause as Dee was brought forward by her students. By then tears were streaming down her face and she was crying and laughing as she wiped them from her cheeks. A loud chant started from her students as they chanted, "Ms. Jones!", "Ms. Jones!" and the audience joined in. Jaxon looked around in awe at all the joyful faces chanting her name. A student came out from behind the stage and presented her with a dozen long stem red roses while the principal joined them onstage and took to the microphone.

"Can we all agree that this musical was incredible?" he shouted, making everyone clap and cheer again. "Thank you to all the volunteers, all the parents of students, to these hard-working students that were up here giving it their all, and last but not least to Ms. Devine Jones, whose passion for the arts made this production possible!" With one final round of applause, the kids dispersed, and the curtain fell again for the last time.

Jaxon turned to his parents and to Barbara and Dex. All of whom had tears in their eyes and giant smiles on their faces. Barbara was the first to speak. "I think it is safe to say, my girl..." she glanced at Dex and smiled, "...I mean our girl is truly something special."

Dex's face was one of elation and pride as he patted Jaxon on the back and leaned into his ear, "Congratulations on the engagement...son." Jaxon widened his eyes and his lips curved into a smile. "We'll talk more later." He continued with a flash of his dimpled smile.

Dee appeared at Jaxon's side, letting out a long dramatic exhale as she held her bouquet of roses. Everyone gushed over her, handing out rounds of hugs and kisses as she vibrated with pride. Looking up at Jaxon, she looped her arm around his waist, turned her gaze to their family and asked. "Who's ready for a party?"

* * *

THE ISLEY FAMILY as well as the community of Primrose had more than outdone themselves with the after party. The large tent was set up in the side yard of the Isley property and was filled with long tables for visiting and enjoying the incredible food. Drew and Cade were busy grilling hotdogs and Rose, along with her friends, filled the tables with delicious snacks and more cookies, cupcakes, and squares than you could count.

"Wow! Your family knows how to throw an after party!" Dee exclaimed, taking in the scene, with an expression of awe and appreciation on her face. "We should mingle, and then I need to talk to my parents." She informed, letting out a disbelieving laugh. "Seriously, I can't believe I can say that now."

"At least you now know your hunch was correct," Jaxon replied. "But I think you all need to talk so that you can get some concrete answers as to what actually happened."

She nodded and intertwined her fingers with his as they made their way from table to table, chatting with students and parents, teachers, and volunteers. Their entire circle of friends was there, raving about the musical and giving them all congratulations and hugs. Savanah embraced Dee for a long time and literally squealed when she saw the ring Jaxon had picked out for her. As they went to chat with Jaxon's brothers, Dee spotted her parents walking up the walkway to the house. Dee squeezed Jaxon's hand, and he leaned down, giving her an ear. "I'm going to go talk to them."

He nodded and brushed his lips to hers for a chaste kiss as he pinned her wary gaze. "It's going to be okay, trust me." She gave him a grateful look and took a deep calming breath before she made her way out of the tent towards the house. *Now is the moment of truth.*

CHAPTER 14

Dee strolled down the walkway, slowly approaching her parents sitting on the front steps of the Isley home, their heads bowed in low conversation. The sounds of her heels clicking on the pavement made them look up, both with looks of surprise on their faces.

"Well, there you two are." Dee said as she reached them and put her hand on her hip. "I believe we're due for a candid conversation." She said, meeting her mother's eyes, then drifting her gaze over to Dex expectantly.

Her mother hesitantly slid over and patted a space between her and Dex. Dee took a seat and put her hands out to both her mother and father. They took her hands, and she let out a long exhale before she started their long overdue conversation.

"Before I begin, I just want to say I'm not angry with either of you. I had a wonderful childhood and you Mom always did your best for me. You gave me every opportunity to grow and thrive in life so I could become the confident woman I am today, and for that I am truly grateful." She said, meeting her mother's eyes and offering her a look of gratitude as she gave her hand a squeeze. "I know there must be a good reason why you did what you did and why Dex was never a part of my life. I know you've been guarded in the past and avoided sharing the full story with me, which in many ways, I completely understand. You felt you needed to protect me and your heart, is that right?" Dee asked her mother. Barbara nodded and turned her gaze to their joined hands. "With that being said, I want the 100 percent truth as you know it from both of you. I deserve to know why Dex wasn't a part of my life and we're not going to leave this step until I have both of your stories and some answers, as well as a plan to move forward."

Dex let out a low chuckle and squeezed her hand. "Loud and clear." he replied, and Dee turned to her mother.

"Mom, I want the truth here. I deserve that much." Dee implored.

"I can do that, my girl," her mother replied, meeting her eyes then going downcast again with a long dramatic exhale.

"I've known Dex was my father for about two weeks now. I first met him through Jaxon and, when I met Dex, I had no idea he was my father. All I knew from our first conversation was that he had once been an actor and we had a mutual interest in the theatre. I visited his shop two weeks ago, delivering his ticket to the show and he and I started chatting about his time in the theatre and why he decided to walk away from acting. Through our conversation, the pieces started to come together and when he smiled, I had a feeling he could be my dad." she shared. "You have to admit I look like Dex, don't I, Mom?"

Her mother smiled a faint smile and replied. "You do. Every time you smiled, you reminded me of him." She confessed, meeting Dee's gaze. "You both have those trademark dimples."

Dex touched his face and looked at Dee, his eyes widening with realization and a smile blooming as she continued. "From the conversation with Dex, I found out he was in the 1997 production of *Dream Girls* and from there, I had my suspicions. Then when I found this picture in the attic…" She pulled the picture of the Cast out of her purse. "…I knew he was my father."

She handed the picture to Dex, and he smiled nostalgically as he held it up to the porch light. "I remember this production like it was yesterday. That was probably the best time of my life," he mused as he handed it over to her mother.

Her mother smoothed her hand over it and smiled too. "It was the best time of my life, too."

"Then I assume you two met when you were both in this cast?" Dee asked to clarify. They both nodded. "And I assume you started dating, a relationship, a tryst, an affair during that time?"

"Dee!" her mother scolded, but Dee held up her hand.

"No, Mom, I deserve to know this story of how my parents met and how I came to be."

"We met during the production, and we were instantly drawn to each other. I had never met anyone more dynamic and beautiful than Barbara, and I was a smitten man. Our first kiss was on stage and sparks flew from there." Dex reminisced, his gaze melancholy as it drifted over to her mother, making her smile as he continued. "My parents were from an affluent family and weren't exactly happy that I chose to be an actor. For years prior to the production, they insisted that I marry a girl from another affluent family they approved of. They continued to try to push a relationship with this girl on me and the girl was persistent as well, but as soon as I laid eyes on Barbara, she was the only one I wanted." he added, glancing over to her mother with a look of longing.

Her mother spoke. "We started a secret relationship from there and fell very much in love with each other. We knew his family wouldn't approve of us dating, so we kept it a secret." Her mother added, looking down at her hands. "Dex proposed to me, but we kept it quiet until we could figure out how to be together."

Dex exhaled and picked up the story. "We continued to see each other in secret, and I loved your mother very much, so we made plans that after the last performance we would run off together and elope. We figured we would get married, and my parents would have no choice but to accept our relationship."

"Explain to me why that never happened." Dee continued. "It sounds like you had a plan, but something must've happened to derail things."

"This is the part where things get vague for me." Dex confessed, shaking his head. "I was ready to run off with you, Barbara. My bags were literally packed, and in my dressing room that night, but then you disappeared."

Barbara sighed dramatically, still looking at her hands

and her mouth turned down, her chin wobbling as she tried to hold back her emotions, but her words came out painfully as she explained. "I went to your dressing room to meet you. I had my suitcase in my hands, and I saw you with her."

Dee turned to her father, her eyes wide and imploring him to explain.

Dex shook his head and looked down, bringing his hand up to run over his head as he cleared his throat and answered. "My parents showed up at the last show and brought the girl they wanted me to marry. I think it was their last-ditch attempt to get me to consider her. When I entered my dressing room, she ambushed me as she told security she was my fiancé. I was furious and informed her that I didn't want to be with her, and that there was no way I would marry her as I was in love with someone else," he informed. "When I sent her off, I went to look for you and you were gone. I couldn't find you anywhere, Barbara."

Dee looked at her mother and squeezed her hand supportively. "Where did you go, Mom?"

Barbara looked up into Dee's eyes, and a tear escaped, rolling down her cheek. "I already knew I was pregnant, and I got spooked when I saw him with that girl at his dressing room door. I was devastated and terrified, Dee. I was 28, and I felt like I had been completely duped. I felt like I had been taken advantage of, and I was old enough to know better. My heart and my pride were in complete shambles, so I ran. I had nowhere to go at first, as all my future was tied to Dexter. We were going to get married and finally be together, so I had already sublet my apartment." She explained. "I had nowhere to live, so after driving out of the city I remembered I had a theatre friend that lived in St. Augustine. I found her phone number and address and called her to tell her what had happened. She said she had a spare room and offered it to me, so I took it. I lived there for a few months until I found a house I could afford with the meager savings I had stashed, and I started working whatever jobs I could find, waitress, receptionist, whatever I could do to make ends meet. I walked away from acting and never went back."

Dee shook her head, letting out a long breath. She turned to Dex, her eyes requesting him to respond. He looked so contrite as he processed her side of what had happened.

"Barbara, I am so sorry you had to go it alone and I want you to know that I would've been there for you if I had known. I loved you so much. I was ready to walk away from my entire family for you. That girl and I were never together and the only woman I've ever loved was you, Barbara. After I lost you, I left acting behind, too. Stepping on that stage never felt the same after losing you."

Her mother bowed her head, burying her head in her hands as her shoulders shook, and she started to cry. Dee wrapped her arm around her mother and Dex rose from the step and took a seat on the other side of her, wrapping his arm around her too.

"Barbara, I completely understand why you did what you did," he said as he pulled her into his chest. Dee let go of her hand and watched as her father consoled her mother, all the pain of the last 28 years coming out in a wave of crashing emotion. She glanced up at her father and smiled, putting her hand on his shoulder. His eyes were so full of emotion and love for both her and her mother and Dee knew in that moment that somehow, someway, they as a family would be okay.

The sound of footsteps on the walkway made Dee look up to see Jaxon coming their way. Strolling slowly, his hands in his pockets and his gaze apprehensive as he approached. He stopped in front of them. "Is everything okay?" he asked, his brows knitted together as he glanced at Dex holding her crying mother and met Dee's emotion filled gaze.

"Yes, J, everything is great here. Let's leave these two alone to talk some more." Dee suggested, getting up from the step and brushing the dust off her dress. "Mom, Dad." she addressed as Dex looked up and met her gaze. "I'll talk to you two later, okay?" Both nodded and Dee took Jaxon's hand as they walked away together, questions answered and the weight of the past just a little lighter.

THREE MONTHS LATER, on a beautiful early fall day, Jaxon and Dee found themselves at the end of an aisle in front of a trellis of cascading fall foliage. *It's a perfect day for a wedding.* Dee gripped her bouquet of white roses, orange dahlias, and daisies, and Jaxon smoothed out the lapel of his tailored suit as their eyes met. Dee gave him a sly wink and smiled widely as her head turned to the back of the church.

Dexter Geoffrey the Third, her father, stepped

forward as the church doors opened and her mother Barbara Jones, stood there looking stunning in a satin mermaid gown with long sleeves and a gorgeous satin rose on her hip. She radiated pure love and joy as she made her long walk to the man she fell in love with so many years ago and never stopped loving to this day.

After her parents reunited, it didn't take long for them to rekindle their romance. They both had held onto the love they had for each other, so once they were finally together there was nothing holding them back. Seeing her mother finally find her happiness filled her with a profound joy she couldn't fully explain. Her mother had made so many difficult choices and had sacrificed so much for her growing up. So, to see her finally be with the one and only man she ever loved was truly beautiful.

Then there was Dex, her freaking awesome dad, whom she could finally start a relationship with, and boy, did he not disappoint. He was smart, funny, loving, and sweet. Everything she thought a father should be and more, and he was beyond excited to have a daughter. They spent countless hours together over the summer, getting to know each other better, and he filled all their lives with so much fun, laughter, and love. She couldn't be prouder to call him her dad and have him in her life at last.

Her mother came down the aisle slowly, her expressive midnight eyes glistening with tears as she reached Dexter. The minister stepped forward and said, "Who gives this woman to this man in marriage?"

"I do! Finally!" Dee exclaimed with a dramatic roll of her eyes and a wide radiant smile curling her lips.

Both of her parents laughed, and Dee took the bouquet as her mother took her father's hands. As she listened to her parents declare their love to each other, she glanced at Jaxon, who stood beside Dex as his best man. He flashed her his endearingly handsome smile, his beautiful blue eyes twinkling with knowledge that in eight short months, this would be them, standing in front of family and friends, promising their lives to one another. She was happy they decided to wait until spring to get married. A time of year that held so many memories for them. With any luck, it would rain on their wedding day. *Isn't it good luck to have rain on your wedding day?* Her mouth curled up into a knowing smile. *I believe it is.*

EPILOGUE

5 years later in Spring

It was a cold, crisp, rainy spring morning and Dee was rocking on the porch swing, bundled in her Isley Construction jacket, looking out on the yard of their new home. A two-story classic country home with a wraparound front porch that Jaxon designed and built just for them, only a mile from where he grew up and two miles from Primrose. They had been here since last fall, but it still felt new to her, like a dream in many ways. In fact, her whole life had felt like one big dream since she met Jaxon. One big, glorious dream she never wanted to wake from.

So much had happened in the past five years. As planned, they had married the following spring, after his grand gesture of a proposal at the dress rehearsal for her first ever Primrose Spring Musical. May 23rd was their wedding day, exactly one year after Jaxon realized that he wanted to marry her. She knew long before him that she wanted to be his wife, but she let him get there at his own pace. *God, that day was perfect.* She sipped from the steaming mug she held, letting the ginger tea soothe her throat and stomach. Their wedding day was everything she wanted and more. Despite always loving the spotlight and taking every opportunity to grace a stage, when it came to her wedding, she didn't want all the pomp and circumstance. All she wanted was a small affair, with their family and closest friends in a place that meant everything to Jaxon and, after their first weekend there so many years ago, was meaningful to her as well. The Isley Lakehouse was the perfect location for their 'I dos'. A place his grandfather built, and where his parents were married decades prior. She would never forget that day for as long as she lived. Walking towards the love of her life, looking devastatingly handsome in his sharply tailored suit, and surrounded by everyone that loved and supported them, they were married overlooking the beautiful lake on a cloudy afternoon. And yes, as suspected, it rained, which made them both laugh at the irony. Of course, even though it was a simple affair, she needed to add her flair to the wedding and make it her own. Opting for a stunning off-the-shoulder red satin gown that showed off her hourglass figure rather than the traditional white. A little bit of drama on an otherwise drama free day. *It really was a magical day.* In fact, their entire relationship had a touch of whimsy and magic. Like Mother Nature herself had played a hand in bringing them together.

The storm door opened, and Dee heard Jaxon's deep rich voice along with the adorable giggles that were always music to her ears. Jaxon appeared looking sexy as always, dressed in his low-slung faded jeans, Henley shirt and Isley Construction jacket. Like a fine wine, Jaxon only got better with age. His dark hair and facial scruff taking on a distinguished salt and pepper that honestly drove her wild. He was still irrefutably the sexiest country boy she had ever laid eyes on.

Jaxon caught her gaze, his ocean blue eyes twinkling as he smiled, his endearingly crooked smile making her heart flutter wildly in her chest. He strolled over and leaned down, planting a tender kiss on her lips. "Hey there, sexy mama," he said, caressing her cheek and kissing her again. He stood up straight and stepped to the side as three pairs of booted feet pattered on the wooden porch. Dee smiled down at their two-year-old triplets, all still in their pajamas, wearing bright yellow raincoats with matching rubber boots. Their cute chubby faces all beaming with excitement and their adorable dimples popping out with their smiles.

"Well, don't you all look like a bunch of little duck-lings?" she said, putting out her arms for a hug. They ran across the porch towards her, and her daughter, Juliet, tripped over her boots only to be caught by Jaxon before she did a faceplant on the floorboards. She started to cry, and Jaxon wrapped her up in his arms, rubbing her back to console her. As her two boys, Dexter the Fourth and Alix giggled and squirmed in her embrace, she watched as Jaxon wiped their daughter's tears away, kissed Juliet's head and set her back down. *He is such a good daddy.*

"Mama." Juliet said, her gaze sad as she swiped at her nose and toddled over to Dee to join her brothers in the embrace.

"Are you okay, sweetie?" She asked, kissing both of her chubby cheeks.

She nodded, her dark tight curls bouncing as she looked at Dee with her expressive midnight eyes. She squeezed her little ones all again, giving them kisses before she let them go scurry off and play in the puddles. Jaxon helped them down the steps and climbed the stairs again to join Dee on the porch swing. Taking his seat beside her, he wrapped his warm arm around her as they watched their children jump and splash in the rain, their giggles echoing across the expanse of their large yard.

I am so blessed. Gratitude filled her chest as she looked at her beautiful children. Having a family was something they wanted as soon as she and Jaxon got married. Knowing with her PCOS diagnosis it would be difficult, they tried the initial fertility treatment with no success and decided to do IVF shortly after her best friend Savanah had her son, Micah. Managing their expectations, they started the process and were shocked when they got pregnant with the first round. Two months later they were dealt another surprise when they found out they were expecting three. After a difficult pregnancy, tense birth, and their babies spending some time in the Neonatal Intensive Care Unit, they were all home, happy and healthy. Jaxon and Dee's life became a blur of bottles, diapers and spit up, but despite the craziness and sleep deprivation, they were thrilled and beyond grateful for their little family. Then as they say, when it rains it pours, just as they had finally settled into a routine, Dee found out she was pregnant again, this time naturally conceived but this time thankfully with only one baby.

"How are you feeling today?" Jaxon asked, his eyes full of compassion as he smoothed his hand over her tiny baby bump.

"Good today. I took a walk and I think the morning sickness is starting to subside," she said, looking up at him affectionately. He smiled and leaned in to kiss her sweetly with so much love and adoration she thought her heart might burst. Breaking their kiss, he leaned his head into hers, their foreheads touching, his eyes locked on hers. "You are so beautiful, Dee, and I love you so much." He said, reaching up and cupping her face. "You have given me everything I could ever want and more."

Her throat tightened with emotion as she looked into the eyes of the man that gave her all of him, even when he was scared, and scarred, and not sure he believed in happily ever after. He took a chance, opened his heart again, and let her in. Their love, just like the unrelenting prairie rain, was steadfast and sure.

"I love you too, Cowboy." she replied with a smile.

With the sweet giggles of their children breaking their revery, Jaxon rose and put out his hand to Dee. Accepting his hand, he pulled her up to her feet and wrapped his warm strong arms around her as he asked, "Shall we go play in the rain, Mrs. Isley?"

Thank you for reading Prairie Rain!
Want more steamy romance set in the idyllic small town of Primrose?
Read Prairie Prestige now!

ALSO BY TANYA RENEE

Primrose Series

Prairie Sky

Prairie Nights

Prairie Fire

Prairie Hearts

Prairie Sound

Prairie Rain

Prairie Prestige

With The Band

Finding Direction

Love Notes

Primrose Series

By Tanya Renee

Prairie Sky

Prairie Nights

Prairie Fire

Prairie Hearts

Prairie Sound

Prairie Rain

With The Band

Finding Direction

The Spring of Love Series

By Virginia Taylor

Forever Delighted

Forever Amused

Forever Heartfelt

The Tooth Fairy Chronicles

By Victoria Rocus

Tooth Decay With A Side Of Fae

Toothaches And Wedding Cakes

Baby Tooth And Tangled Roots

Wisdom Tooth And The Awful Truth

A New Page

by Aimee MacRae

It Happened in Paris

By Michelle Beesley

The Bondi Bubble

By Megan Krolik

White Butterfly

By Kim Foale

The Ancient Fire

By Ellen Read

The Love Healer

By A. K. Leigh

For more information visit:

www.serenadepublishing.com

ABOUT THE AUTHOR

Tanya Renee is a proud Canadian Prairie girl, who grew up on a family farm in Southeastern Manitoba Canada. Always an avid reader, she became intrigued with the romance genre at an early age when she first read Romeo and Juliet. Soon after she started to craft her own stories and poetry and by the time she was in high school, she had declared someday she would become a writer.

Married to the love of her life, she resides in Steinbach, Manitoba Canada with two teenagers and a menagerie of pets. When she's not cooking up a storm in her kitchen, she can be found tinkering in her garden, drinking copious amounts of coffee with a book in hand, listening to 80's music/audio books or at her laptop creating stories that are emotionally satisfying. She writes what she wants to read, epic stories that bring you on a journey and make you believe in love.

www.tanyareneeromance.com

ACKNOWLEDGMENTS

Firstly, I need to thank the librarian who first allowed me at the age of 10 to take out William Shakespeare's Romeo and Juliet from the school library. If I could remember her name I would share it, but I truly believe that reading this classic Shakespeare play fostered my love of romance, drama, the arts, and my love of literature and poetry. Thank you for answering my questions and explaining parts of it to me as well as encouraging me to read more of his work. Educators like you make a difference.

I want to thank my wonderful drama and choir teacher, Mrs. Shirley Reimer, for allowing a shy young girl to be part of the productions. Even if I couldn't act or sing a lick.

I want to acknowledge Landmark Collegiate who inspired the backdrop for this story. The level of excellence this school has maintained with their musicals has never failed to entertain the community. Well done!

Thank you to my mom, who shared her love of old movies and musicals with me. Some of my favorite memories are watching them with you. Love you!

To my husband Bart for his constant support and my awesome kids, Theo and Raina. I love having you as part of my hype team.

And lastly to my publisher, Serenade Publishing, for believing in me.